# DREAMQUEST

## JANET WELLINGTON

LOVE SPELL  NEW YORK CITY

LOVE SPELL®

May 2004

Published by

Dorchester Publishing Co., Inc.
200 Madison Avenue
New York, NY 10016

ISBN 0-505-52592-5

The name "Love Spell" and its logo are trademarks of Dorchester Publishing Co., Inc.

Printed in the United States of America.

Visit us on the web at www.dorchesterpub.com.

# PRAISE FOR JANET WELLINGTON AND *DREAMQUEST*!

# FOUND!

He was definitely exotic-looking: long, black hair, skin bronzed by the sun, and a smooth, broad chest and flat stomach. His entire body looked tough and powerful. There was even an inherent strength in his face, with smooth skin stretched over high cheekbones, a straight nose; and the set of his chin suggested a stubborn disposition rather than a dangerous one. But his dark eyes betrayed something else, something familiar. Darkly intense eyes, eyes that seemed to hide pain, perhaps—and secrets.

A shiver raced up her spine, which created a chill over her entire body, along with a severe feeling of light-headedness.

"Are you here to rescue me, or are you just a voyeur?"

Special thanks to my editor, Chris Keeslar, for seeing something special in this book of my heart, and much gratitude goes to my agent, Linda Kruger, for her abiding support.

Thank you to my own Robin, who has an incredible knack for dream interpretation, and to Carol, who has patiently waited for this story, all the while assuring me that it would find a home.

Thanks to my husband, Jim, for sharing that "what if" moment that launched this story, for assistance with historical research, and for introducing me to the wonder and beauty of the Anza-Borrego desert. And to my voraciously reading mother, for demonstrating the way to sanity and relaxation can indeed be found in the pages of a good book.

This book is dedicated with respect to the Indians of San Diego County: the Kumeyaay, Luiseño, Cupeño, and Cahuilla.

And finally, to you, dear reader: May all your happiest dreams come true.

*"Go confidently into the direction of your dreams!
Live the life you always imagined."*
—Henry David Thoreau

# *Prologue*

The boy stood at the mouth of the cave, his body trembling from the physical effort required to remain erect.

*Háawka, Hattepaa kwa'stik.*

He cocked his head and lifted both hands to cup his ears, then stopped his breath. *Not* breathing came as a relief from the shortened, labored gasps his breath had become over the last few minutes. Was the voice real, or had he just heard it in his mind? Another cruel hallucination?

"Hello, Little Coyote. I am here."

The clear sound of his grandfather's voice dissolved the doubts and unanswered questions he'd battled during the difficult journey. His heart sang. Grandfather was there and waiting for him, just inside the cave. He shuffled forward but paused after only a few steps, fatigue threatening to buckle his knees. He concentrated as he reached deep within to find the strength to continue.

The cool air inside the cave was the first sensation he had allowed himself to feel in days, and it was a soothing wind against his hot skin. Then that wind seemed to slip under his feet, making it possible to take the dozen more steps he knew he needed to take in order to save his life.

For two days he'd controlled pain, thirst, and hunger as he'd made his way to where he believed his grandfather would be.

Two days of accepting every sign without question.

Two days of taking each path as it was presented.

And on this moonless night, without hesitation he'd approached the rattlesnake and allowed it to strike. And just as Grandfather had foreseen, he'd been like an observer. He'd watched the snake leap toward him, feeling but *not* feeling the fangs sink into his thigh. Just for that instant, that moment, it was as though he had not been in his own body. And though it had seemed like a dream, he'd known even then it was deadly real.

"Tell me, Little Coyote, why you are here."

"I have met *'ewii taaspiich*, and he has sent me here to test you."

The old man nodded; then his creased, sunweathered face softened with a broad smile. Bringing his pipe to his lips, he puffed on it until a blue cloud of smoke surrounded his head. He set down his pipe, lifted one hand and patted the rabbitskin blanket spread on the ground next to the glowing embers of a low fire. "I will show you, grandson, so that you will believe."

As his grandfather helped him recline, Coyote watched the old man examine his wound. Blood had trickled from the bite and dried, and redness surrounded it.

"With the bite of the snake, it is done," his grandfather whispered.

The old man began to sing a slow chant and add branches to the fire, and soon sparks showered the ceiling of the cave as the embers grew into tall flames. From Coyote's waist, he unfastened a small gourd that hung by a braided rope, undid the lid and peered inside.

"When did you drink the *tolvaach*?"

"Before the sun came up today." Coyote groaned, his body restless with the pain he no longer denied.

Grandfather dipped a bowl into a large storage *olla*, then brought it to Coyote's parched, cracked lips.

"My *'aaskay* is filled with sweet water for you, my grandson. Drink and tell me what you have seen and heard. Tell me of your dreams."

"The dream—it was the *same*, Grandfather. Even after drinking the *tolvaach*. It was the same."

"And you hoped for something different?"

"Yes." He'd assumed his quest would change

3

everything. He'd believed the dreams would finally end, or at least new dreams would come to him. Dreams that were clearer, dreams he could understand.

"You cannot control these things."

"But why is the dream the same?"

"It *isn't* the same."

And suddenly he knew Grandfather was right. Nothing was ever the same. He needed to look more closely, to be less impatient. "Will you tell me what these dreams mean? What is to happen to me?"

"Yes, *Hattepaa kwa'stik*, it is time for you to know."

The old man picked up a long white feather and began to chant. He brought the tip of the feather next to the boy's wound, then drew it along his skin in long, gentle strokes.

"Grandfather, will this feather heal me? Is this feather from the white bird of my dreams?"

The old man frowned and renewed his chant. After several minutes, he paused. "The white bird in your dreams is a white woman."

Coyote moaned and lifted himself onto his elbows. Anger surged through him, and intense pain followed close behind. "No!"

Coyote's grandfather pushed his hand firmly against the boy's chest, and forced him to lie down. "Listen to me, grandson. Soon a white girl will come to you in your dreams, and she will take the white bird's place."

"Tell me why."

The old man nodded his head. "Listen to what I have to say, *Hattepaa kwa'stik*. I rode the wind two suns ago to save this girl. Now, it is you who are destined to keep her safe."

"But—"

Putting a finger to the boy's lips, the old man quieted any more questions. The rising monotone of his chanting echoed against the walls of the cave as he continued to stroke the feather along the boy's entire body.

Finally, Coyote stilled. He drifted away from consciousness, sinking into a state of relaxation far from the pain and fear and poison that threatened his life.

He stared at his grandfather's face through half-closed eyes and tried to focus on the lips. He could see they were moving, but the words were too soft. With the last of his strength, he strained to hear what the old man was saying. And a moment before he floated away, he thought he heard one word, the one his grandfather's lips had been forming: "*Kuseyaay*."

Shaman.

# Chapter One

"Robin, are you there? Please pick up if you're there . . . it's Suzanne. . . ." She waited, her pulse racing. *Please be there . . . please be there.* Finally, she heard a click that interrupted the beep at the end of the answering machine message.

"Suze, I'm here—what's going on?"

"I had the dream, but this time I remember some of the details. You said to call—"

"Indeed, I did. Have you written it down yet?"

"You said to *call.*"

Robin's voice dropped to a whisper. "Just a minute. I've got . . . company."

"Oh, jeez, Robin. Why did you pick up?"

"You should have heard the sound of your voice. You would have picked up, too."

"Sorry. It's just that I've never remembered this much and—" Suzanne listened to muffled voices, guessing her friend had put a hand over the mouthpiece of the phone. She should have waited. Glancing at the clock, she groaned. No wonder Robin sounded half asleep. It wasn't even seven yet.

"Okay, I'm back."

"Robin, I'll let you go—"

"Forget it, he's gone for a jog and he'll be gone at least an hour. I'm all yours now, so start talking."

"I'm sorry—"

"Say it again and I'm hanging up."

"Right. Okay. Well, it started the same. At least I think it did, because usually I just don't really remember the beginning part and—"

"Suzanne Lucas, just talk it out! Leave your blasted logic in your left brain and let your right brain do the communicating, okay? Now, breathe . . . then start. Repeat after me: At the beginning, I was . . ."

Suzanne took a deep breath, grateful for the guidance. "Okay. At the beginning, I'm young—maybe fourteen or so. The young guy wasn't there in the beginning of the dream. I open a door and then all of a sudden I'm in a cave—but it becomes a tunnel and I follow an old, gray-haired Indian out into the open. He's showing me some pictographs he just painted on a wall."

"Good. Tell me what they are."

Suzanne closed her eyes to take herself back to the dream. It was already getting fuzzy, and felt more and more distant as the minutes passed. "I'm losing it, Robin."

"You have paper and pencil there? Sketch

while you're talking to me—we can do this," she encouraged.

Suzanne took a pad of paper from the kitchen counter, found a pencil in a drawer, and began to draw. "A circle, and it's kind of spiderwebby inside the circle." She paused and brought the eraser to her lips. "And lines stuck out all around the circle."

"Like a sun?"

She stared at the symbol she had drawn on the pad. It *was* like a sun. "What does it mean?"

"We'll come back to it later. Any more pictures on the wall of the cave?"

"Two hands; one black and one red."

"The outline of hands?"

"No. More like you would put paint on your hand and make a handprint. They're next to the sun-thing—and then two stick people. One's black and red and white. The other's red, but with white lines coming out of the head."

"Like the sun-thing?"

"Yes, actually."

"Okay, and what were you and the old man doing?"

Suzanne pinched the top of her nose, then pressed on the inner corners of her eyes. Her head had started to throb a little from one too many margaritas the night before. The celebration had been a total act of coercion. She'd tried her best to argue that the festivities were premature, but her esteemed fellow faculty had successfully ignored her. She'd finally given in to the happy hour soiree, figuring her colleagues needed an excuse for a party and her enviable new job offer certainly fit the bill. After a couple of drinks, she'd managed to at least temporarily bury her dislike of public jubilation, especially when it made her the center of attention.

They had toasted her good fortune and praised her eminent worth through countless pitchers of margaritas, until the manager of the Cantina Diego finally shooed them all home. And during the evening, each had confessed his professional jealousy. But they'd also said they believed no one deserved the opportunity more than she did.

When they'd challenged her hesitation about immediately accepting the job, they'd shaken their heads, bewildered. Each claimed he'd do almost anything for the chance to start an ethnobotany department anywhere—but especially at the small private college in northern California recruiting her. None would ever understand that part of her would give almost anything *not* to have to move a thousand miles away, even if it was for the perfect job, the job she'd dreamed of all her life.

"Suze?"

"I'm here. Let me think. I don't remember the old man talking to me . . . just him showing me the paintings. Then—oh, and he kept touching my hair. Does any of this make sense?"

"Keep talking. I'm taking notes."

"Then we go back through the tunnel and out the other side. I remember seeing a full moon, and a rabbit drinking from a pond. And then the old guy stops and pushes me forward . . . and the young guy's standing by the water. I'm older now . . . pretty much the age I am right now, I think. And the young guy seems about the same age as me, maybe a little older."

Suzanne looked at her pad of paper. Below the pictograph symbols she'd drawn a simple landscape; a pond surrounded by fan palms, and a full moon in a shaded sky. It looked like something a child would draw. A feeling of déjà vu brought chills to her skin, and she had the distinct feeling she *had* drawn it as a child.

"Suze?"

"Sorry—got side-tracked for a minute. So, he's standing there. I still can't see his face—I can't really see him clearly at all. I just have sort of a sense of him. Tall, good build . . ."

"But, the *same* guy from your other dreams, right?"

"Yes, I'm sure of that part. I just wish I remembered more about what he looked like. Every time I've been to the Barona reservation, I feel like there's a chance I might run into him, you know?"

"Anything else?"

"Well, I remember something flying just above our heads, and when I turn to look, it's an owl.

When I turn back, both the young guy and the old man are gone. And then I woke up and called you."

"Okay, I've got my laptop right here. Give me a minute to pull up a web site I want to check."

As Suzanne listened to the clicking sound of her friend's fingers on keys, she realized it was the most she'd ever remembered about a dream fully awake. Through the years she'd found that if she kept perfectly still after she woke, it was like she was still there—with everything crystal clear, her senses still filled with every sight, sound, and smell. But the minute she moved or opened her eyes, her precious dream world faded.

"Almost there," Robin said.

Cradling the phone against her shoulder, Suzanne pinned her drawing to the bulletin board, just above the offer letter from the University of Spring Lake. She ran her fingertips over the gold-embossed image at the top of the letterhead: several peak-roofed buildings surrounded by tall pine trees. A forest surrounded the elite private college, and it was about as far from San Diego as she could get and still be in the state of California.

She should take the job. It offered her both the challenge and the opportunity of a lifetime, and it was a logical next step for her career. And her career *was* her life. As a student, she had discovered the blessed sanctuary of university life, and she'd stayed in the environment through graduate school then landed a teaching job.

Her life was completely on track.

Yes, she loved teaching. Her existence within the milieu of higher education was logical, dependable, and predictable. And it perfectly suited her every need. She'd worked hard to have something tangible to hold on to that belonged only to her, and deep down, she knew exactly what she should do. And she'd have to give them an answer, and soon.

"Okay, Suze, I'm ready. I wanted to check a site that has Native American symbols so we could compare your dream symbols to them."

"Okay, dream guru, tell me what you think."

"The first pictograph—the sunburst—could be a supernatural sign, like something a shaman might paint. Handprints are also considered magical—symbols of strength, and for keeping evil spirits away."

"And the stick people?"

"It's the colors that seem most important. The one that's the combination of colors indicates someone of high status—a chief or a healer, maybe. I think the red one with the white hair might be you. Red is a sacred color, usually female, and I think the white hair is important. In your dream you said the old man kept touching your hair, right?"

"Yeah." Suzanne tried to run her fingers through her long, wavy hair, a tangled mass of blonde curls she hadn't bothered to braid before she fell into bed last night.

"In dreams, hair symbolizes physical and spiritual strength, and it can also refer to knowledge and reasoning. I think in your case, it symbolizes you to him."

That seemed logical. "And . . ."

"And the whole idea of you walking through a door *into* the cave is very interesting. Doors are passageways, sometimes from one plane to another, or from one state of consciousness to another."

"Don't go woowoo on me—"

"Hush," Robin interrupted. "And so, when you go through the door into the cave—which I interpret as a place of refuge or sanctuary for you—when you go through, you are passing into this symbol of safety and maybe to a new life. Then the old man takes you outside to the pond, right?"

"Correct."

"The only symbolism I could find for the rabbit was lack of personal awareness. And the full moon is there to make you feel secure. The moon is also feminine energy . . . and sometimes means romance and passion. So tell me, girlfriend, *has* there been any *romance* between you and the young guy in other dreams? Have you been holding out on me?"

Suzanne stared into space. She considered whether she was ready to share the intimacy that had escalated in her dreams as she and the boy had grown older. She'd been dreaming of him for so long. No. Too private. Too intimate. "Another day, Robin."

"Hmmm. Okay."

Suzanne listened to the sound of more keystrokes, then Robin continued. "Ah . . . the owl is considered the eagle of the night—meaning change is on the way."

"Well, *that* makes sense." As usual, her friend's interpretation seemed to contain a grain of possibility. Robin was the only one she'd ever confided in about her vivid dreams. For years she'd kept them hidden, dismissed any meaning that might be in them and simply enjoyed them for what they seemed to be: her only real creative outlet, and her sanctuary. The first time she'd mentioned her recurring dreams, Robin had listened with serious concentration, and Suzanne had used the word *obsessed* instead of *enjoyed*. It was kind of embarrassing, she'd confessed that day, to have a part of her prefer her dream world to her reality. But Robin had been fascinated and made her promise from that moment on to tell all details of her dreams when she remembered them.

"So what if you have to stretch that logical mind a little and believe in the unbelievable?" she'd said. They had been close friends ever since, and Suzanne's friendship with Robin had been the only other constant in her adult life besides her career.

"So, you *are* taking the job, right?" Robin asked.

"I'll let you and everyone else know for sure when I get back from the desert."

"Taking your favorite students on another plant identification field trip?"

"No, we're on break. This trip's just for me."

"Might be the last one for a while, huh?"

Suzanne didn't want to answer that. "What about you—you still leaving, or have you come to your senses?" Her heart still ached from Robin's announcement she was following the current love of her life to New York to support his acting career.

"Life's supposed to be about taking chances, Suze."

"But you're sacrificing everything for something completely uncertain!" Her words were followed by the sound of Robin's cheerful laughter, so loud that it forced her to pull the receiver away from her ear for a few seconds.

"Someday," Robin said, "even *you* might have the opportunity for adventure. Not everything can be wrapped up in some nice little package the way you like it."

Suzanne shook her head. "I happen to believe that most things can be. Besides, you haven't even known this guy that long."

"Contrary to your belief system, sometimes people do fall completely and totally in love in an impossibly short period of time. You've just had some bad luck over the years."

"I don't think I'm destined for long-term relationships. It just never fits quite right."

"Luck changes sometimes."

It was their oldest argument. Suzanne didn't believe in luck; she believed in taking an active role in one's life, and it had served her well. "I'm just afraid you'll get all the way to New York and things won't be what you expect."

"Then I'll do something else." There was a pause. "Why are you being so miserable about your best friend's happiness, anyway?"

Suzanne nibbled on her lower lip. Robin was exactly right. She should be happy for her, and she knew that. It just seemed so dangerous to give in to love or lust or whatever her friend was in. *Too* dangerous.

"Hey—the dude's back," Robin cut in. "I gotta go. Call me when you get home from camping—promise?"

"Of course. And Robin . . . ? I am happy for you, you know."

"I know."

"And thanks for the dream analysis. It's always interesting."

"My pleasure. Talk to you soon."

Suzanne hung up the phone and headed for the shower. These days before the start of the summer semester offered her the invaluable gift of time, and a solitary camping trip to her beloved desert would provide the safe seclusion she craved. Even though she knew in her heart of hearts what everyone thought she should do, there was something else calling to her. She didn't know what, but everyone would just have to wait a few more days.

With binoculars in hand, Suzanne stepped out of her tent. The rocky red vistas that surrounded the Borrego Palm Canyon Campground always took her breath away. Carefully adjusting the focus, she scanned the sides of the mountains, but there wasn't a bighorn in sight. Either they were getting more and more scarce, or her eyesight was getting worse. She hoped for the latter—or maybe the sheep had learned to stay more out of sight, out of danger.

The likelihood of their scarcity alarmed her, and if more than half the nation's population truly lived on the rocky slopes she stared at, the sheep were probably in trouble again. She made a mental note to check at the Visitors Center on her way back home for the current stats of the rare animal. She felt truly obligated to keep herself informed, and not just for her students' knowledge, but more for the stewardship she felt for the park itself.

Her gaze shifted above the rocks. In vivid contrast to the rugged rusty peaks, the sky was a clear, almost impossibly bright blue. Cloudless. Smogless. So beautiful. And it promised a spectacular night sky. Even with the full moon the stars would be dazzling, and the Milky Way would be a wide snowy streak across the heavens.

She breathed deeply, slowly. It felt so good to be back. And, as always, there was that indescribable something in the air that replenished her; or maybe it drugged her—a happy desert addict come home again—and she wished it could be forever.

It perpetually amazed her that even though she'd probably stood in this same spot over a hundred times through the years, it always seemed different. Something always changed. Plants were larger, or absent if the winter had been especially dry. There were more desert critters, or fewer. Nature always changed the desert, and yet the essence of what she loved about it never changed, and it was that enduring feeling that drew her back again and again.

The bits and pieces she remembered of her desert dreamworld also motivated her to spend time here. And she'd discovered that it was when she was in the desert that somehow she was able to look beyond herself a little more easily. Over the years, she'd realized that her thinking was better, clearer here than anywhere else on earth, especially when she was hiking.

With sunset still a few hours away, she had plenty of time to squeeze in a short hike. And the walk would serve to prolong the welcome tranquility that already blanketed her. Hopefully, it would extend well into the night. Often she struggled to sleep the first night out here in the desert—too saturated with energy and enthusiasm to relax. A hike would tire her out a little so she might get a decent night's sleep, making it easier to get up early for a long day of contemplation about the university job offer.

Her stomach tightened at the thought of the trip's real purpose. The decision she would make would affect her more deeply than anyone could understand. She knew she shouldn't be having second thoughts, but she was.

"But you understand, don't you?" Her gaze followed a red-tailed hawk as it soared through the azure sky and floated along the ridge on its four-foot, russet-colored wingspan. Then the hawk tipped its wings and caught a strong thermal rising above the hot desert floor, providing the lift for which it searched. The majestic raptor circled skyward, eventually disappearing from view.

Reluctantly, Suzanne pulled the binoculars from her eyes. She'd gladly trade places with the hawk. She envied the aerial view that always provided him with the proverbial big picture, something that sometimes eluded her—especially in times like this, when her heart and head disagreed.

Suzanne stepped back into her tent to tuck the binoculars into their case, and picked up her jacket. Reconsidering, she dropped it back on her sleeping bag. It was still warm, and she'd be back long before things had a chance to cool down. The temperature all day had been hot but comfortable, only in the low nineties instead of the triple digits more typical for early June. And according to the last report she'd heard from the radio on the drive in, the nighttime temperature should be a comfortable sixty-five degrees. She'd be fine in her sleeveless top, jeans, and hiking boots.

Outside, she glanced around as she zipped the tent door shut. She still had no neighbors. The campground had been pretty empty when she arrived, and she'd had her pick of sites, quickly settling on one of her favorites. It looked as though this trip she wouldn't have to suffer from nearby tents of partiers with their kegs of home-made beer, radio-controlled cars, or endless bocci games. She'd had her share of visits in the past when the state park filled up with weekend warriors determined to bring the city with them: campsites devoid of hiking boots and backpacks and, instead, filled with portable hammocks, flip-flops, and stereos. Over the years she'd learned to camp during the week when she could, just to avoid the assault of people and noise in the sacred place she selfishly claimed as her own.

She grabbed a bottle of water and walked toward the Borrego Palm Canyon trailhead. As she walked, she stretched her neck from side to side and tried to work out the tension that still lingered there. Pausing at the mouth of the trail, she extended first one leg, then the other, stretching each against a giant granite boulder. Then she bent over at the waist and dangled there, stretching her spine, hoping the last remnant of stress would leave her body.

Her head still hanging, she looked between her feet and watched a zebratail lizard first dart between a barrel cactus and a tiny fishhook cactus, and then skitter beneath a brittlebush. After several deep breaths, she finally pulled herself upright. A few torso twists, and she was ready to begin.

With the first step onto the trail, she made the conscious decision the walk would be less destination-oriented and more a meditation of remembrance. The mile and a half of gently winding trail tended to be her first hike when visiting the 600,000-acre park. It never failed to spark a sense of nostalgia, taking her back to her childhood and cherished memories of walking with her foster parents to the native palm grove oasis at the end of the trail. When her adoption was finalized and her new mother and father asked her to choose an official family trip, it was the Anza-Borrego Desert State Park that she'd chosen without hesitation. It had remained her most favorite destination.

Setting a leisurely pace, Suzanne walked the well-groomed path and stopped often to check on favorite plant specimens. The large ocotillo had responded nicely to the wetter-than-average winter season. More than a foot of rain had been recorded since December, and it certainly showed.

She stepped off the trail to get a closer look. The plant had sprouted many more long stems from its base, and the single spines on each stem were longer, the remaining leaves greener. Intensely red flowers tipped every long stem and witnessed the moist season, and the plant towered over her with vibrant growth. She shook her head, wishing she had brought her camera. The ocotillo had never looked healthier.

Next she crouched at the sign that marked a cheesebush and rubbed the stem between her fingers, then sniffed the pungent aroma that gave it its name. She couldn't walk past her favorite plant without stopping for the age-old ritual.

She continued, delicious memories washing over her, and she became keenly aware that this particular walk would generate its own new memory. It could very well be her last trip to the Anza-Borrego Desert State Park for a long while. With that thought, concentrating on the sights and sounds grew in importance, and she didn't want to be casual about anything she saw or smelled. Every image was filed away in her mind for later retrieval. Could she ever feel this way about the pine forests where the University of Spring Lake was nestled?

Pausing at a bend in the path for a water break, she leaned her back against the cool, rough surface of a huge boulder. When she pulled the bottle away from her mouth, the air stilled, and there was a very odd and total absence of sound. The songs of the birds and even the faint rush of the stream had faded away to nothingness. She looked up and down the path. There was no one in sight, and she hadn't passed anyone on the path since she'd started. There had been no sounds of other hikers since she'd been walking, only the crunch of her footsteps on the trail.

A roaring sound pulled her attention upward, and as she looked at the lofty rock walls that surrounded her, she noticed puffs of dust along the face of the cliffs. A rumbling sound gradually built, and then a slow, rolling vibration began under her feet.

*Earthquake*?

The water bottle slid from her hands, and Suzanne headed in a dead-run back toward camp, her heartbeat pounding in her ears. Rocks showered down around her, and she felt an impact on her head. She needed to get away from the cliffs, get back into the open and hope for the best.

Dust filled the air, and soon forced her to stop. With her fingers shaking, she managed to untie the bandanna from around her neck so she could cover her nose and mouth. Her eyes stung from the dust and she felt sweat dripping down her forehead and trickling between her breasts.

She pushed on as she dodged falling rocks and debris, and tried desperately to keep her feet under her as the earth continued to shake. Finally she reached the trailhead and looked toward her camp.

But there was no sign of her tent. Or her car. Nothing was where she'd left it. Had she taken a wrong turn?

The rumbling resumed as a strong aftershock began, and she spun around to see huge boulders sliding down the face of the cliffs.

She turned again to where she should see her tent, and squinted at the scene that now appeared instead. A man and a woman stood next to a silver teardrop trailer still hooked up to an old Buick. They seemed to be screaming and pointing toward her—no, *past* her toward the face of the mountain. When she turned to look, a small girl of maybe five with long blond braids, stood frozen between two large boulders, her eyes huge with fear. Suzanne stared in horror as a fist-sized rock bounced through the air directly toward the little girl's head.

"Look out!" Her scream was quickly lost in the thunder of the aftershock, which seemed even more violent than the initial quake.

But suddenly, out from behind one of the boulders near the girl stepped a gray-haired man, bare-chested and dark-skinned, wearing a simple loincloth. *The old man from my dreams? Impossible.* Suzanne shook away the thought, blinked hard, and prayed the scene would change to something normal, something that made sense.

In one smooth motion, the man caught the little girl just as she was struck by the rock but before she could crumple to the ground.

Suzanne gasped, and a repressed memory of the moment filled her mind in a painful flood. *That was me . . . that happened to me!*

She stared open-mouthed as the old man turned toward her for an instant, and their eyes locked. In her mind she clearly heard his voice.

*You will always be safe.*

Then he looked up the mountain and ran, the child limp in his arms.

Dust clouds billowed everywhere, clogging the air and, with Suzanne's next breath, her lungs. As tears streamed down her cheeks, she hugged her ribs and coughed violently.

What had just happened?

Then, not listening to reason or logic, she climbed up the face of the mountain toward the trail the old man had taken. Without any rational grounds, she knew she must follow him.

# Chapter Two

Though the old man couldn't have been more than a hundred yards ahead of her, Suzanne never caught up with him.

As she followed, she kept the bandanna over her nose and mouth to minimize inhalation of the dust-filled air, and concentrated on the rocky path to keep from turning an ankle or falling. Periodically she looked up and caught glimpses of the back of him, his gray hair loose and hanging well past his shoulders. More than once, he paused and turned as though to check on her progress. Eventually she lost sight of him as he rounded a huge boulder, and when she reached the spot, she stopped. There was no sign of the man, and the primitive path she'd been following had all but disappeared.

The last of the rumbling had ended, and the air was much less choked with dust and fine rock powder. Suzanne wiped her face with the bandanna, then leaned against the side of the boulder to try to get her bearings.

She'd never strayed from the groomed path when she'd hiked the palm canyon trail, and her elevated position—now up above the base of the mountain—gave her a confusing perspective. Everything looked wrong, the way places she'd only seen in daylight could look so different at night. Suddenly navigation became an uncertainty.

And the air felt strange too. Thinner? Silkier? No, it just felt *empty*.

As she closed her eyes, Suzanne resisted the urge to rub them and instead hoped tears would kick in and wash away some of the stinging particles. She remained motionless against the boulder for a long time, until her heartbeat eventually returned to a normal pace and she felt calmer.

She focused her attention on the silence, ready to run if the earth beneath her feet started shaking again. Then in a rush, sounds resumed: a lizard-like rustle in the brush, the sharp *keeahrrr* of a hawk. Sounds of life. Even the wind returned; it whispered past her and through the canyon.

To stimulate tears Suzanne opened her eyes and blinked hard, then dabbed at their corners with the bandanna. As she surveyed the immediate area she confirmed that, unfortunately, nothing had changed. She'd actually fantasized that when she opened her eyes she'd look down on the familiar well-groomed nature trail . . . and a search party. *No such luck.*

She retied the bandanna around her neck and stood away from the boulder. Resting her hands on her hips, she considered her options.

The old man definitely had headed in the general direction of the oasis when she'd lost him. There she could at least wash her face in the pool, and rest comfortably. And from the vantage point of the palm grove, she'd more easily find her way back to the regular trail and then back to the campground.

*If it still existed.*

She ignored her growing apprehension and doubt, and after a final look toward where she'd come from, she turned and continued toward the towering palms she could just see in the distance.

She studied the ground in front of her as she walked, acutely aware of where she placed each foot, and watchful for any movement that might warn of an approaching snake. The animals would at first be as dazed as she after the quake, and then they'd be more likely to be active. It had been a pretty big jolt; she guessed at least a six and a half magnitude and, judging by the size of the boulders that had rolled down the cliffs, with an epicenter in very close proximity.

The temperature cooled as she neared the grove where dozens of native fan palms stretched toward the sky. Even in the fading light she could see blooms at the tops of the trees, the whitish clusters of flowers predicting a heavy crop of fruit to come. It was a comforting sight. A familiar sight.

Suzanne quickened her pace, and when she reached the pool she dropped to her knees and soaked her bandanna in the water. She wiped the grime from her face, and next squeezed water over her arms, noticing several scrapes and bruises she must have gotten from the sprays of rocks that had hit her during the beginning of the quake.

Licking her dry lips, she resisted the urge to drink a handful of the water, fearing giardia and the gastrointestinal distress that would invariably develop within hours of drinking what her studies forced her to assume was contaminated water. Still, she felt a little better, unsure if it was the coolness of the water on her skin or the fact that at least, at that moment, she knew exactly where she was.

The light dimmed even more as the sun slipped behind the mountain, and she shivered, goosebumps forming on her damp skin. Suddenly she wasn't so sure she should go back toward camp and, besides, what would she be returning to?

Sitting back on her heels, she stared at the water and weighed the alternatives. She should probably rest, but she felt more self-assured and less helpless while she was moving. Plus, she had no provisions for spending the night, no emergency food or supplies. She should go back.

Satisfied with her decision, she added the thought that, logically, her campsite would be right there this time. Another shiver motivated her to stand and turn away from the pool to begin the trek back.

The mouth of the trail was precisely where she'd thought, though a great deal of rubble covered the once-smooth path. The light was better, too, away from the palm grove, and even without the benefit of the full sun she could see her way clearly.

As she pushed forward, she ignored the feeling of foreboding that disturbed her sound reasoning. *So what if the path looked quite a bit rougher and the plant markers had disappeared altogether?* After that big an earthquake, many things would have been changed; signs would have toppled and could easily have been buried in the rubble.

After walking for several minutes, the cliffs gradually fell away and the desert floor expanded in front of her. By her estimation, she should be nearing the beginning of the trailhead, and just within view of the campground.

Her heart sank as she looked into the distance. Nothing. No camp. No familiar restroom building. No people. Nothing was the way it should have been.

She dropped to sit on a flat rock, and tears filled her eyes. She wasn't sure what she'd expected to see: her little tent, *or* the odd scene of a younger version of herself, and her foster parents standing next to that trailer she'd instantly recognized. But there was nothing. Had she really seen them? Had it all been just an hallucination? A vision? Or maybe it was some sort of repressed memory somehow recalled by the powerful shaking of the earth?

*But what about the old man?* She was sure he was the same she'd seen in her dreams over the years; he looked so familiar. And she could still hear his deep voice in her head. Could that have been part of the vision, too? She was doubtful.

Her tearful gaze moved from the open area to the mountain and back again. It had all seemed so real, almost like a snapshot from a family album. When she'd watched the little girl crumple to the ground after the blow to her head, the whole scene had felt painfully real. Good sense totally argued against it, but her whole being was stuck on what she still felt inside.

To finally remember that day—at least the beginning of that day—amazed her. At least now she actually recalled the earthquake that had happened when she was five. But that was all she remembered even now, the rest was still a blank.

*So what had really happened?*

She thought about her foster mom, and the years the woman had put up with her endless requests to tell about the fateful camping trip. The recounting had remained her favorite bedtime story throughout childhood. So, no matter how small or confusing, regaining at least a piece of her past comforted her. When she got back to San Diego, she'd have to write to her foster mother and check on the accuracy of some of the details of the setting, and what she'd just witnessed.

But, what now? Should she stay, or go back and try to find where she might have strayed from the path? Weariness forced a sigh from Suzanne, weariness that stemmed from the combined exertion of the hurried hike and also from simple nervous exhaustion.

She thought about the old man's words: *Always safe.* There wasn't much she wouldn't give at that moment to feel safe again. But more than that, she felt she had to *do* something—even if it meant walking, when a big part of her really wanted to just sit there and cry her eyes out in frustration.

Pushing herself up from the rock, she turned to retrace her steps, to check for a fork in the path that somehow she'd missed. In her heart she sensed the futility, but the logic of it was far too inviting, too comforting. She wasn't ready to admit she was either lost or, worse yet, that somehow things had unexplainably changed.

After three more unsuccessful attempts at a new outcome, she resigned herself it would be best to return to the oasis and stay put. Thunderclouds had gathered while she made her attempts to find the right path, and she didn't relish the idea of spending the night with no shelter from the rain. She'd noticed a small cave close to the pool, a good place to wait out the storm. A safe place.

Turning toward the grove once more, she walked, moving her gaze between the trail and the stormy sky ahead of her, watchful for a glimpse of the tops of palm trees.

As she peered into the mouth of the cave, Suzanne's eyes gradually adjusted to the dim light. The space was roomier than it appeared from the outside and would provide quite a nice shelter.

Taking a fallen palm frond, she used it to tap in front of her as she entered, hoping any critters inside might be encouraged to leave. Then, careful not to grasp the thorny edges, she used the frond to sweep the floor of the cave, her final attempt to rid her abode of any remaining creepy-crawlies. Returning outside, she gathered more fronds, then dropped the makeshift bedding in a spot close to the mouth of the cave but far enough away that the rain wouldn't reach her.

The stack of fronds wasn't particularly comfortable, but they would provide a decent barrier to the floor of the cave. She'd just gotten settled, sitting on the thick layer of crunchy leaves, when a few large drops of rain began to fall. The June shower would be welcomed by the harsh desert environment, and the unexpected moisture might even cause a few late flowers to miraculously push to the surface or to sprout from a cactus or two.

Everything would look brighter in the morning. She drew her lips into a forced smile. The optimism was really aimed more toward her predicament than her environment. She dismissed the thought, and instead focused on disconnecting from her emotions, hoping to feel more in control. It was her most tried and true defense mechanism, and had served her well through her early childhood in the foster-care system and the years of waiting for her adoption to be approved.

She took a deep breath and dropped into teacher mode, reaching for her knowledge base of desert survival. Shoving her hands into the pockets of her jeans, she took inventory: a miniature pocket knife, a tissue, half a box of Tic Tacs. She clenched her jaw, unable to avoid mentally kicking herself for not grabbing her daypack for the hike. It contained a carefully packed emergency kit complete with bright orange poncho, a drop sheet and parachute cord, her favorite Swiss Army knife, some waterproof matches, a mini flashlight, a compass, and water purification tablets: Everything she needed and wished she had.

She popped a Tic Tac into her mouth, dumped out the rest into the palm of her hand, and counted what was left. The cool taste of peppermint relieved her thirst temporarily, and she blessed each of the nineteen mints that remained. She returned them to their plastic container and snapped the lid shut.

Looking around, she evaluated her shelter. Dry from the rain, it had no apparent signs of animals. Secure enough. But the lack of drinking water was definitely a problem.

*Stop. Think like a survivor.*

"Okay, Ms. Lucas." Her voice filled the silence as she spoke out loud in her best cranky-teacher voice, as a favorite student had dubbed it. "Recite the seven-point Air Force survival checklist." She made two fists and held them out in front of her, ready to pop up a finger with each step. "First, positive mental attitude; then first aid, shelter, fire, signaling, water, and food."

She felt great comfort in the structure the list provided, and since she considered her attitude as good as it was going to get, she skipped ahead to the second point and began to inspect her scrapes and bruises more carefully. Her left shoulder had begun to ache, and when she reached back to slip her fingers under her tank top to rub it, she discovered a large tear in her top and what felt like a pretty nasty gash along her shoulder blade.

Next she held out each arm, turning them to see all sides; several more scrapes, a particularly deep one on the back of her left forearm. The legs of her jeans showed no rips or tears, so she figured the sore spots she'd noticed were only bad bruises. Her fingers wandered over her face and neck and finally to her head. There she felt a good-sized tender spot on the top, and when she brought her hand back, there was fresh blood on her fingertips.

"*Great*. A head injury, and serious scrapes on the upper back and arm." She considered walking out into the rain to cleanse the wounds, but reconsidered after she thought about having to spend the night wet and chilled, with no tools to make a fire. She'd see to her wounds in the morning.

Next on the list? Signaling. *Signal whom?* There hadn't been a sign of anyone since she'd run toward the old man and away from the bizarre scene at the campground.

Next? Water—the Earth Mother's blood. She eyed the rain that now dripped from the mouth of the cave as the shower intensified. *I should be catching the rain!*

Bounding to her feet, she looked around for anything she could use to catch the rain. The curved woody stems of the palm fronds would make lovely shallow troughs. Pulling the knife from her pocket, she cut the palm leaves away from several particularly bowed stems. As she finished each one, she placed it just outside the entrance of the cave, keeping some inside to act as reservoirs.

She watched anxiously, waiting for enough rainwater to accumulate so she could pour off the excess into one of her storage troughs. One full; now two. Then, as quickly as it had started, the rain diminished to a soft drizzle.

Two would have to do, and certainly the ounces she'd managed to catch were a vast improvement over none. She settled back onto her palm frond mattress and had a celebratory Tic Tac while she waited for any sediment in the water to settle to the bottom. Finally, she lay down on her stomach close to one of the troughs to drink her reward, not wanting to risk spilling any of the water by lifting the container to her mouth.

The taste wasn't too bad, but she wouldn't have complained if it had tasted like pond scum. She had hydrated herself, and that was significant. Water would be vital to help keep her head clear and to avert poor judgment, the biggest enemy to anyone trying to survive in the wilderness.

She eyed the remaining trough. "Tom Brown, Jr.," she said in an exaggerated announcer's voice, "as one of the world's most respected outdoorsman, I ask you—Should she drink it, or save it?" She paused, then dropped her voice an octave. "Survival tactics dictate you should store as much water in your stomach as possible. She should drink!"

Suzanne emptied the second trough, forcing herself to drink more slowly. In the morning she could look for natural rain catches in the rocks or even collect dew if she had to, but at that moment, her body felt a thousand times better with precious fluid back inside.

Night had fallen and, for the first time, Suzanne felt secure enough to relax a little. She returned to her palm frond seat, then stretched her arms and yawned. It had been a hell of a few hours, and she felt completely wiped out.

*Be careful what you ask for.* The thought popped into her head, unbidden. She *had* wished she could stay here forever, and she'd wished it many times over the years—practically every time she'd visited the Anza-Borrego desert and especially every time she'd ever camped here. A shudder emphasized her realization that, this time, it seemed her wish had a possibility of coming true.

Leaning on one hand, she dropped to her less injured right side, then curled up on her makeshift mattress. She should try to get some rest. More than ever she hoped that while she slept she would enter her desert dreamworld; maybe there things would make sense and, at the very least, she'd have the comfort of a safe and familiar place.

As she slowed her breathing and tried to turn off her thoughts, she listened to the sounds of the night, surprised how safe she felt. The high-pitched musical trill of nearby toads and the rolling *churrr* of woodpeckers consoled her even more; a lullaby of night noises. Identifiable, normal sounds. Sounds she expected to hear.

She concentrated on long, deep breaths until she drifted into that mysterious place between wakefulness and sleep where all seemed well. Then, at last, she let go, sinking into a heavy slumber.

"Mes-haalyap."

*Opening her eyes, Suzanne removed her sunglasses and turned her head toward the deep-timbred voice that found its way through to her consciousness. She had fallen asleep stretched out on one of the chaise lounges by the swimming pool of her apartment complex, an open textbook resting on her stomach. Her heavy bath towels tumbled in the dryer, the multi-tasking providing her with much-needed reading time.*

*An elderly man sat in a chair next to her, an orange-and-black butterfly resting on the tip of his forefinger. She stared at it, not even bothering to look at the man's face to see if she knew him. She was afraid to breathe; afraid to ask him to repeat what he'd said; afraid that if she spoke, she'd be the one to cause the monarch to flutter away.*

*She sat motionless and watched the butterfly's wings gracefully open and close in a dance on his fingertip. Periodically, the monarch's black antennae dipped and gently touched the man's finger as though it were some strange new plant.*

*"How do you do that?" she whispered, finally unable to repress the question.*

*"I am a friend to mes-haalyap, so there is no need for it to fear me. I am simply a tree branch or a rock to it."*

*Suzanne drew her lips into a contemplative line.*

The butterfly could simply be lethargic, one of the leftovers trying to migrate north or, perhaps, with its breeding complete, it had stopped for some nectar, then was too weary to continue and waited to die.

"You should stop thinking," he said, "and put out your finger."

She obeyed, amazed that the butterfly didn't fly away. Then he brought the creature to within an inch of her finger and, after a quick flutter of its beautiful wings, it hopped from his finger to hers.

She brought the monarch closer, within inches of her face; a rare opportunity to examine the fairy-like insect. She could almost imagine an expression on its face. The butterfly flickered on the end of her finger and then launched itself into the sky. She watched until it fluttered out of sight.

Turning to her companion, Suzanne stared into his dark eyes. They were like liquid night, were eyes that seemed to probe her very soul.

"That was amazing," she said softly.

"There is beauty everywhere you look," he agreed, his gaze turning upward to the cloudless blue sky before returning to look at her.

"Do you live here?" She searched her memory, certain she would have remembered the man and his leathery, tanned skin and long gray hair. He shifted in his chair, and she had the impression he was more than slightly uncomfortable in his green and blue plaid shirt and dusty jeans.

Or perhaps it was her open stare. She dropped her eyes.

"No," he said. "Just visiting a friend."

*Suzanne nodded her head, unable to find words; unexpectedly mute. She felt overwhelmingly at peace, though. For no reason, his presence seemed to send a wave of serenity that dissolved any feeling of nervousness or indecision. It felt good just to be next to him.*

*Then he eased himself up and out of his chair, and offered her a wide smile before he turned to walk away.*

*She wanted to follow him, but immediately dismissed the idea as absurd. Instead, she picked up her textbook again. She had some serious reading to do, as this was only one of many books she was studying for the curriculum she was writing.*

*After rereading the same page for the third time, she gave up and put the book down. Her head just wasn't in it. Pulling her tee shirt off over her head, she took a few quick steps and dove into the pool.*

# Chapter Three

The chilly water soothed her hot skin, a welcome relief to the raging fever that had awakened her. After running from the cave and hastily shedding her clothes at the shoreline, she'd stepped into the pond and immersed her body in the cool water, determined to lower her body temperature as quickly as possible. It was almost dawn, and she'd spent a fitful night.

She walked into the water until her feet could no longer touch bottom, then breast-stroked to the middle of the pool. She stopped, treading water so she could look around. Satisfied she was still alone, she stretched out and drew her legs to the surface so she could float on her back.

She concentrated, struggling to hold on to the wisps of dream that still floated in her mind. She'd been home . . . *home.* And something about a butterfly.

*And the old man again.*

The thought ricocheted in her head, causing

her eyes to pop open. She stared up at the tops of the tall palms, and tried to analyze what she remembered. She'd been by the pool, he'd put a butterfly on her finger, and then he'd left. That was it. *Robin, where are you when I need you?*

Closing her eyes again, she fought unexpected hot tears. It was probably just the fever that made her feel so emotional, weak, and unable to clear her mind. *Relax.* Her wounds were probably just a little infected, and soaking in the water should take care of getting them clean and, with luck, slow the infection until she could get some first aid.

She kept her eyes closed, replaying the dream images in her mind one more time. There had been something more . . . a connection of some kind with the old man. It definitely felt like there was something else, too, but she just couldn't retrieve it.

*Let it go.* She forced her arms to relax away from her sides, and she only permitted herself to think thoughts that had to do with the coolness of the water and the weightlessness of her body.

Coyote's sandaled feet made no sound as he turned in the direction of the palm grove. It had been a long and tiring night of walking so that he would be in time to see the first light of day dance on the water, as Grandfather had insisted. A long and tiring walk, but a good one; a walk of preparation. Grandfather's instructions had been explicit: *Arrive at the palms just as the night*

*departs and the new day is born, and return to me
when your life is no longer the same.*

"*Enyehaa,*" he whispered, "my water." It certainly wasn't *his* water, but at that moment he
felt that if somehow the water could take a physical form, its life force would indeed flow
through his veins and provide him the strength
he would need for his quest. The water—the
Earth Mother's blood—held everything he
needed for the rest of his journey.

Just as the palms came into view, a streak of
white pulled his gaze to his left. A bird sailed
past him, and Coyote's eyes followed it until it
disappeared among the trees. *Was it a message?*
He shook his head in disgust—if it was, he
didn't want it. He'd had enough years of recurring dream images, first of the white bird and
then the faceless white woman. He hoped with
all his being that *this* time, *this* quest would cause
the images to leave him. He was ready for answers, and Grandfather had promised he would
have them.

With familiar landmarks coming into view,
Coyote knew he was close to the oasis and quickened his pace, eager to make camp in the cave
by the water. As he reached the cave's entrance,
on the ground he noticed a few palm stems with
the leaves removed, and just inside, a neatly
stacked pile of palm fronds.

He sniffed the air as he entered the chamber.
No sign of a campfire. No aroma of food. He
dropped his belongings to the ground and

spread a rabbitskin blanket on one side of the space. With care, he leaned his willow bow against the opposite smooth wall. Next to it he placed a quiver of obsidian-tipped arrows, then he set down a bag filled with food-gathering essentials and tools. Last, he placed a woven basket that held the rest of his supplies—some dried rabbit and fish, a supply of acorns and seeds, and his medicine bags.

A shaft of weak sunlight shone into the cave, and Coyote straightened his back. *First light.* After a swim in the pond to wash away the dust from his journey, he'd evaluate the immediate area for fresh food to supplement what he'd brought to sustain himself for the duration of his stay.

As he walked outside, he saw the white bird again, this time standing motionless at the edge of the pool. It had returned.

And just beyond it was . . . *someone in the water.* Coyote dropped to the ground to get out of view, then raised his head to look again.

A woman.

How had he not noticed the white woman in the water when he'd arrived? He heard a clear whisper in the recesses of his mind, his grandfather's voice. He'd heard it often in the days since he began his quest.

*Do not question this, for it is indeed the white woman you are destined to protect.*

Pulling himself up to his knees, he crawled silently to a hidden vantage point behind a rock.

Concealed, he studied the woman. Hair the color of corn silk floated in long wavy strands away from her head; rosy-tipped breasts extended from the water, and her relaxed arms floated perpendicular to her body, her legs slightly apart.

He was powerless against his own animal reaction to her naked body, maddened by the immediate intense effect her physical beauty had on him. Were her eyes the color of the sky? Or dark like his? He stared at her with a strange mix of both curiosity and hostility. He didn't want her there, especially now. She would be an irritation at best, a hindrance at worst.

She still hadn't moved a muscle, though he could see the shallow rise and fall of her abdomen. Seemingly so completely at rest, he wondered if she was asleep. Then he noticed the scarlet of her cheeks; by the looks of it, she had a fever. *Smallpox*? The possibility was quite real, and quite deadly. His stomach filled with the burn of contempt and loathing for her and all her kind. Destiny or not, if she was ill with the smallpox, why should he help her? It would be a betrayal to his tribe and the memory of his mother and father. And a betrayal to himself.

This white bird—white woman, he corrected himself—was sure to be only trouble for him and for his people.

He crept closer to look for lesions on her skin or any other telltale signs of disease. She drifted in the water, still unmoving, coming nearer and nearer to his new post behind the trunk of a large palm at the water's edge.

His perusal started at her feet, and moved upward. No signs of sores. As far as he could see, her legs were completely free of blemishes, though he did notice bruises on her thighs. His eyes followed her legs to where they ended at slightly rounded hips, and his stare paused at the triangle of golden hair where her legs joined—and again he felt his arousal beneath his loincloth.

He looked skyward, determined to separate from the unwanted feelings his body exhibited. After a few moments, his gaze dropped again to her body, and he continued his scrutiny—over her stomach, and then her breasts. Still no sign of disease.

Looking at her neck, he saw a rounded vee of browner skin that matched the brown of her arms and legs, all a vivid contrast to the much paler skin of her torso. He had seen this coloring of white skin before, but it surprised him to see the pattern on this woman. He'd seen it on the working whites; typical for a farm wife, perhaps, but, somehow this woman did not have the countenance of someone who tended fields or livestock.

She floated, now, less than two arms' lengths away, and he looked more closely at her face. No marks or sores, only unnaturally red cheeks. Her brows pulled together, and then her forehead wrinkled as though she were puzzled or dreaming. Her eyes moved beneath her pale eyelids, and he felt certain she was lost in a dreamworld after all.

Reluctantly, Coyote stepped out from behind the tree to wait for her eyes to open.

Suzanne tried to clear the fog in her head. She tested her memory by trying to decide where she was . . . exactly. *Floating. In deliciously cool, fresh water.*

She opened her eyes just a crack to peek at her surroundings for clues. Her blurry gaze moved down from the top of a palm tree and landed on a man leaning against its trunk, arms folded against a muscular bare chest; long hair draped in front of his shoulders. He seemed . . . *what*? Stately—like the trees—and steadfast. She smiled at the old-fashioned word.

He didn't move, just stared at her with dark, probing eyes. Eyes like the old butterfly man. They resembled each other a little, those two—only this man was much younger.

*Ah, my dream man. . . .*

Her eyes closed again, and she was happy to be dreaming and wondering where the dream would take her. She moved her arms a little, which sent a sharp twinge through her left shoulder that pierced the fog. *Damn.* The pain instantly dissolved the dream, and memories surfaced of the earthquake, the injuries, and the fever.

Bringing the back of her hand to a cheek, she

confirmed her fever still raged, which also confirmed she should probably take another look at her wounds. She opened her eyes and turned her head toward the shore, her gaze resting on . . . the man leaning against a tree.

Suzanne submerged her body, accidentally gulping a mouthful of water in the process. She turned away from the shore, choking and sputtering until she successfully cleared her airways.

*Please be gone when I turn around. Please be just a feverish hallucination, a leftover bit of dream. . . .* She turned her body in the water and returned her gaze to the shore. The man was still there.

She dropped her feet to the bottom so she stood in the water, her arms crossed over her chest, with just her head and shoulders above the surface.

"Are you here to rescue me, or are you just a voyeur?" she asked. A wave of mild annoyance at his silence had washed over her.

She inspected his expression: first a furrowed brow—*a tiny smile?*—and then only a blank stare. He didn't appear to understand her. But why wouldn't he? She supposed he could be Spanish-speaking; Mexican? But somehow she didn't think so—his features were more angular, almost regal.

"Do you speak English? *Hablas inglés?*" she asked, forcing confidence into her voice. Though she felt completely vulnerable, she'd be damned if she would show it. She waited, but there was no change in his face, no sign of recognition or comprehension of her words.

He was definitely exotic-looking; long, black hair, skin bronzed by the sun, and with a smooth, broad chest and flat stomach. His entire body looked tough and powerful. There was even an inherent strength in his face, with smooth skin stretched over high cheekbones, a straight nose; and the set of his chin suggested a stubborn disposition rather than a dangerous one. But his dark eyes betrayed something else, something familiar. Darkly intense eyes, eyes that seemed to hide pain, perhaps—and secrets.

A shiver raced up her spine, which created a chill over her entire body, along with a severe feeling of light-headedness. "My c-c-clothes," she stammered, her teeth chattering uncontrollably. She pointed to the rock where she'd left her things and pantomimed pulling a shirt onto her arms, hoping he would understand.

His eyes followed the direction of her finger and he even took a step toward the rock, leaning to look at the ground behind it. But he shrugged when he turned again to face her, shaking his head a little from side to side.

"I'm f-f-freezing and I've g-g-got to get out of the water." She took a step forward, rubbing her arms and hugging herself. "Look, y-you t-turn around and I'll get out and get my clothes myself." She uncrossed her arms and pointed at him, then stirred a circle in the air with her downward pointed finger; finally putting her hands over her eyes and rotating her own body in the water to try to make him understand. When she turned again to face him, he had turned his back to her.

Relieved, Suzanne slowly walked toward the shore but kept her body low in the water. Either her fever was breaking or she was getting worse. Her head had begun to pound fiercely, and she feared she was really ill.

Her shivering increased rapidly as she gingerly stepped out of the water, her teeth now chattering violently. She clenched her jaws tightly to prevent them from clicking together, determined to maintain control at least until she was able to get dressed. She kept her gaze on the man's back until she reached the rock, then looked down to where she was certain she had dropped her clothes. Only they weren't there.

"Oh, n-n-n-no—where *are* they?" As the words left her mouth, a darkness crept over her awareness, and Suzanne felt herself falling into a black tunnel. She recognized the symptoms and had a vague idea she was about to faint. It was as though she no longer had full control over her body; her thought processes seemed intact, but her brain felt disconnected from her skeleton and her muscles. Then, as if in slow motion, she felt her knees give way underneath her. Just before she crumpled to the ground, she felt a smooth, strong arm beneath her knees, another along her back and coming up under her arm.

The darkness, not quite complete, was swiftly closing in. She used her last ounce of control to pull her head up, and through heavy-lidded eyes, met the black eyes of the stranger. Eyes that gleamed like glassy volcanic rock—*obsidian?*

She held on for a moment longer to try to measure his expression. They were compelling eyes, assessing eyes—*a rescuer's eyes?*

They were dark eyes filled with shifting stars, but somehow she felt—no, she knew—that these eyes belonged to someone who meant her no harm.

# Chapter Four

Coyote carried White Bird back to the cave. The woman was already creating trouble for him, and he clenched his jaw in irritation. As he bent to enter the cave, he adjusted her body in his arms, and her head flopped against him. Where her cheek touched his chest, his own skin instantly blazed with heat. She had a serious fever and he needed to act quickly. At least for the moment, she was his responsibility.

He gently placed her on her back on the rabbitskin blanket he had spread next to the shallow fire pit, and then began his examination of her wounds. Before she'd collapsed he'd noticed the serious abrasion on her left shoulder, and there were probably other injuries. His fingers traveled over her legs first, lifting them, bending each at the knee in order to thoroughly inspect her skin for bruises or open cuts. As his fingers moved over her body, he felt her stir against him. Her hands reached up to rest on his shoulders, and he pulled her up against one of his extended arms to better examine her shoulder and back. The scrape he found on her back was deep, and it oozed infection. He also noticed a bloody area on her head, and he ran the pads of his fingers over the bump there.

"I've missed you," she whispered, her eyes still closed as she tipped her head back, away from his touch. She turned away, then lifted her hand to put her fingertips on his cheek.

Coyote stared into her half-closed eyes and saw liquid blue irises shimmering with fever. And as he searched her expression, he watched her lips curve into a tiny smile. Wiggling out of the restricted position, she freed her other arm until both hands rested on his face. He barely felt the featherweight touch of her fingers as they caressed his cheeks, then his jaw. Then she drew his mouth to hers.

When their lips melted together, Coyote allowed himself to fall into the warmth he found there, and for a long moment he was lost in the soft, tender kiss. He felt her heartbeat pound then quicken against his chest, and she moved even closer to him until he was unable to feel any separateness from her. She deepened the kiss as she wrapped her arms around his neck.

The growing heat of her body so close against his, forced him to break the embrace, pushing her gently back against the blanket. Her eyes closed, but her mouth remained in a wide smile as she drifted off into a deeper sleep.

Coyote gazed at her. How could she kiss him with such passion and such . . . familiarity? And how could he return her kiss so easily? This was a white woman! He watched her sleep for a few moments, then pulled the sides of the fur blanket over her, hoping the added warmth might help break her fever.

Reaching for his medicine bag, he dumped out the contents to check his supplies. He would need to gather some fresh materials to augment the minimal dried medicines he'd brought, certain he would need to treat her for several days.

A mellow rolling *coo-c-o-o* sound pulled Coyote's attention from the small deerskin bags of dried herbs, and he looked toward the mouth of the cave. An owl perched on a flat rock just outside. It was small, less than a foot in height, earth-brown in color with white spots and a dark collar around its throat. But it was the bird's eyes that he took note of most: black-rimmed golden eyes that glowed beneath white feathered eyebrows. And those golden eyes stared at him, unblinking, piercing.

*A message was coming.*

Coyote quickly began to gather what he needed to collect fresh plant supplies. He dumped the bundles of dried meat and seeds from a woven basket, then inside he placed a digging stick and various cutting tools.

The palm-strip basket was strong, though many years old. Running his hand around the rim, Coyote remembered how, when he was a boy, Grandfather had insisted he at least try to learn how to weave the twisted strips. It would be a useful skill, he'd explained, and Coyote had sat for days with one of his peoples' best basketmakers. He'd kept the basket all these years, and had added handles only recently, before this journey began. Now, it would be perfect for the task of plant gathering.

After one last look at the woman, Coyote gripped the basket's handles and turned to leave. The small burrowing owl had disappeared, and in its place, a white-winged dove paced on the flat surface of the large rock close to the pond.

"Ah, perhaps you have come to help me with this White Bird who is so sick." Coyote tipped his head to one side, and stared at the dove. Within seconds, its wings fluttered and the bird took to the air.

Coyote kept sight of the dove, following it a long distance away from the cave. As he ran, he offered many silent prayers that he would find the plants he would need and a good harvest. Finally the narrow pathway widened into a vast region filled with desert plants. He walked to a large area filled with low, spreading beavertail cactus. And though it was too late in the season for the lavender-colored pads to flaunt their showy magenta flowers, they were already forming fruit. He would remember the spot and return to collect it in a few weeks, after the fruit had sweetened.

But that wasn't what he needed now. Selecting

the largest stand of cactus, he broke off young joints with his stick, rubbed each pad in the sand to remove the tiny spines, then placed the cleaned flora in his basket. He would need many—some pads for the pulp he would use to heal the woman's cuts and wounds, and extra for food. Now he would be feeding two. He worked for several minutes until he was satisfied with the number he had cleaned and stowed.

As the last of the cactus pieces were secured for the trip back to the oasis, he sniffed the air and turned to see a large creosote bush several yards off the path. Though his medicine bag held adequate dried creosote leaf powder, he could use some fresh stems and leaves. Crushed and soaked in a small amount of water, they would serve as an added pain reliever that could be rubbed on the woman's skin. Though she hadn't shown any terrible discomfort, he was certain the pain would be fiercer as soon as she was more alert.

The creosote bush was small, only about three feet in height, but it was lush with small yellowish-green leaves. Its flowers, too, were long gone, and tiny fuzzy white fruits were developing. The rains had been good this season, and the desert had become a garden filled with food and medicine. He cut several small branches and added them to his basket.

In the distance was a shrub of dull, green, leathery leaves. *Jojoba*. As he got closer, he saw there were many dark brown, fingernail-sized fruits on the plant, and he gathered as many as he could, filling the remaining spaces in the basket with the hard, acorn-like fruit. After they were roasted, he would crush the jojoba fruit to extract the soft insides from which he would make a salve to treat the woman's head wound.

Next to the jojoba a large ocotillo was in full bloom, its long, spiny, whip-like stems towering above him. He guessed the plant's base was at least three arms across, each thorny, mostly leafless stem taller than three men. A smaller one stood behind it, the scarlet blooms on the ends of the stems easily within reach. Coyote popped a flower into his mouth to measure the sweetness, then gathered handfuls of the red blooms and wrapped them in a thin piece of deerskin to tuck into his basket. Mixed with water, the blooms would create a tasty and sweet drink, a treat for himself as well as the woman.

Satisfied he had everything he needed, Coyote secured his tools at the top of his basket. He stood and slowly circled, his eyes taking in every detail of his surroundings, establishing landmarks and inventorying key plants he would remember to harvest on his next visit, and judging when other plants' flowers would turn to seed that would provide even more nourishment.

In the distance he could just see the very tips of the palm trees. Camp was far, but he knew exactly where he was and he felt an odd mixture of well-being and anticipation. His quest already had changed.

He heard the sound of his grandfather's musical laughter in his mind, rippling through his arms and legs and filling him with unexpected waves of joy and relief.

*Grandfather?*

*Yes, Coyote.*

*Why has it all changed?*

*Nothing has changed.*

*My quest is interrupted by this White Bird.*

*Your path is the same.*

He was ready to admit he had fooled himself into thinking he had known what to expect when he'd left the village. He'd been so sure he would at last learn precisely what his purpose was and what his life meant—to his people, to Grandfather, to himself, and to the Earth Mother. He smiled after a few moments; his first lesson had begun and he now knew every step of this journey was an answer in itself.

After a deep breath, Coyote raised his hands, reaching his fingertips toward the darkening sky until he felt he could actually touch the wind that rolled off the mountaintops. In a loud voice he thanked the owl and the dove for leading him so quickly to the plants he'd needed to treat the woman's injuries, knowing valuable time had indeed been saved. Then he thanked each of the plants for their generosity in sharing of themselves—and their power—in order to allow him to heal the stranger.

With a final long prayer—this one to his grandfather, to thank him for sharing his knowledge of healing, for teaching him the secrets of listening to the Earth Mother—Coyote raced back to the cave. To White Bird.

Coyote sat on a rock near the cave's entrance to prepare his first remedy. He laid out the beavertail cactus pads and scraped some pulp from each open joint into a small wooden bowl, then cut up the flat pads into small pieces he would boil in water for a later meal.

Carrying the bowl filled with pulp, he entered the cave. In her restlessness, the woman had thrown the blanket off and turned over so she was now lying on her stomach. He knelt next to her to look more closely at the scrape on her back. The wound there was raw and infected, with another serious abrasion that almost ran the length of the back of her left arm. Both wounds were surrounded by inflamed, reddened skin. He was glad she slept; the pain would have been great had she been alert and feeling.

He dipped two fingers into the bowl and spread a thick layer of pulp on both injured areas. Reaching for a strip of thin deerskin, he finished up by wrapping her arm to keep the salve from being rubbed off; then he took a much longer, wider piece and managed to secure it by wrapping it against the large wound on her back under her left arm and then over her right shoulder.

She groaned when he lifted her up in order to encircle her with the dressing, and he winced, sharing her pain, surprised at his empathy for her. Fate was here, just as Grandfather had predicted. For now, he would not question his role, though other questions continued to surface. How was he to seriously pursue his own quest with this white woman to care for, an injured woman who might be very slow to heal?

*Grandfather?*

*Remember all that I have taught you, Coyote, for this is also a test of your skills. Remember well, or this woman will not live. And she* must *live.*

Coyote closed his eyes to listen for more of Grandfather's voice in his mind, but he heard only silence. It was as he'd feared. The wounds were serious enough to be life-threatening, and now he would need to focus only on his medicine bag and the lessons he'd learned.

The woman moaned, and he lay his hand on the small of her back to still her, hoping his touch might comfort her, let her know she was no longer alone and that he was there to fight for her life.

After a moment, she began to relax beneath his touch.

*'Aaw.* He needed fire, and quickly. Every other remedy he intended would require boiling water.

He waited until the woman had completely quieted, no longer moaning or thrashing, her breathing finally deepening to indicate she had drifted far away from consciousness. The dressings would provide relief and allow her to rest and begin to heal. She would sleep for a long time.

Coyote lifted his hand from her and reached for the quiver resting against the cave wall next to his bow. From it he pulled a long and narrow bundle that had been tucked in with his arrows: his hand drill and hearth. With it, new fire was only minutes away; without it, his own survival became more difficult, and the woman's fate grim.

Unwrapping the bundle, he spread the fawn skin on the floor of the cave and picked up the drill. He ran one hand along the long, pointed stick, checking for any unwanted moisture. He had made the hand drill on one of countless visits to the oasis, visits he had made when he was a boy as Grandfather taught him all the things he needed to know.

Grandfather had chosen a thin piece of dried palm fruit stem for him to make his first drill, and he'd worked for hours on it, rubbing and rubbing one end of the long stem against a stone to fashion a point. When he'd brought his efforts to his grandfather, the old man had looked at it, shook his head, snapped the stem against his raised knee and handed him a new one. The point had been too thin and sharp, he'd said—try again.

He'd been furious at his grandfather's criticism, had stormed off, spending the rest of the day shouting at the rabbits and the hawks and any animal who would listen to his anger. Then he'd tried again, and again he'd failed.

One last time he'd tried; this time more slowly and without anger. That third time, Grandfather had smiled when he'd run his large rough hand over the smooth surface of the drill, his thumb and two fingers caressing the blunt point his grandchild had fashioned. Without a single word of praise, Grandfather had simply begun teaching the next step: making the hearth.

Again he'd handed Coyote a piece of dried palm fruit stem, this piece two times wider than the one for the drill. Then he'd shown him his own hearth; a flat piece of wood just over a foot in length and a little less than an inch wide, with several hollowed out areas, each having a narrow groove that ran from the depression to an outer edge of the wood. Grandfather had handed him an obsidian knife to work with, and Coyote carefully gouged three sockets into the hardened and dried flat piece of wood, and then carved a notch from each to the edge. He'd worked slowly and painstakingly, determined to complete the task right the first time.

When he'd presented his work, Grandfather had felt each hole with his finger then frowned. "Too deep, Little Coyote, and it is impossible to put wood back in." He'd casually tossed the piece into the fire and handed him a new blank. Holding his tongue, Coyote had requested to see Grandfather's hearth again and then asked to keep it so he could check his work while he carved out the sockets. Grandfather had shrugged and left him alone, without hesitation entrusting him with his most valuable possession.

All day Grandfather was gone, finally returning at sunset with two small white-throated woodrats draped over his belt. Coyote had worked all day at a pace so slow he thought he might go mad. First he'd touched the sockets of Grandfather's hearth with his eyes closed until his fingertips memorized the depth and shape of them, memorized the slope of the shallow impressions, imagining the dull point of his own drill spinning inside.

Then he'd stopped to consider that his grandfather's drill and hearth were old, ancient really. And it was then that he'd understood he needed to fit his own new drill to its own shallow impressions in the flat wood. His drill and hearth had to be right for each other, and not necessarily the same as Grandfather's. The holes in his hearth needed to suit his own new drill.

Both would, over time, look more and more like Grandfather's but now, at that moment, he would have to carve, then check, then carve tiny amounts more until the sides of the dull point of the drill sloped just the right distance away from the sides of the hearth's impressions. The grooves were not as complicated, simple narrow channels that would entice the beginnings of fire to travel along them to the finely shredded inner bark of willow that waited, a pile of precious tinder on the ground that would become the miracle of new fire.

He had learned the lesson well.

Coyote returned his attention to the task at hand, which was to make a new fire for White Bird. "Thank you, Grandfather." He whispered the words as he moved his tools closer to the shallow pit where he would make a fire that most likely would not be extinguished until he left the cave to return to the village of his people.

Stepping outside to look for firewood, he spotted a dead creosote bush near the pool, and he soon carried back an armful of dried branches. First he arranged several large stones that would serve to hold a water vessel for heating, and placed them to one side of the fire pit. He needed one more trip outside for tinder—with no willow available, fine dry grass would do.

Back inside, he knelt, one knee securing each end of his flat hearth. He crushed some of the grass so it was almost a powder, sprinkling some into one of the channels that ran between one of the sockets and the edge of the hearth. The rest of the fine grass he put in two piles on the ground, one pile just at the end of the groove, the other close by. Then he put a pinch of sand in one of the depressions, followed by the pointed end of the drill stick. He held the drill between his open palms, leaned his weight onto the drill, and spun it. He twirled the stick back and forth, deftly moving his hands from top to bottom and back to the top again until wood powder formed and browned in the socket. Then a wisp of smoke appeared, and the beginnings of fire traveled along the notch to his grass tinder.

Coyote blew softly into the bundle of tinder, then added more grass, finally picking the pile up in his hands to continue to blow on it. Just as the glowing ember became a blaze, he placed the handful of fire into the pit, quickly adding small branches to feed the flames.

As he continued to coax the fire by adding bigger and bigger pieces of wood, he placed two water vessels on the stones he had positioned on the edge of the fire, then dropped a handful of jojoba fruit close to the base of the fire where they would roast. When he looked up for a moment, he found the woman's eyes open and staring at him. He wasn't certain she was fully awake or aware; the life-force in her eyes seemed weak. But she licked her lips as though she wanted to speak and was having difficulty finding her voice.

"You made a fire . . . with a stick." Her voice came out in a coarse whisper that he barely heard. She licked her lips again and said, "Everything hurts. . . ."

He went to her, and as he knelt down and touched her cheeks, her gaze didn't waver from his. Her skin still blazed with fever—he needed to prepare the next course of treatment. With the back of his hand still on her cheek, she closed her eyes and again drifted into a restless sleep.

Back at the fire, in one vessel he added dried cheeseweed buds to the water to make a tea that, if he could get her to drink it, should lower the woman's fever. In the other vessel, he added to the water the tender leaves and slender branches he'd gathered of the creosote bush, then took a thick short stick and mashed the leaves and stems within it. If that didn't work to lessen the pain, he'd try a wash of black sage.

He stared at the fire, then poked at the jojoba fruits, finally scooting them away from the coals. He scooped them out of the fire using a carved wooden spoon, and placed them into the shallow of a granite mortar slab. He palmed a small stone pestle and lightly began to grind the jojoba fruits, breaking away the hard outer shell so he could make a salve of the flesh inside for the woman's head wound.

His confidence grew as he expertly prepared his remedies and planned ahead the other things to try if she worsened. He remembered all that Grandfather had taught him, and now the lessons had an even greater value. This he knew. But beyond the task at hand—healing White Bird—he knew nothing about what was in store for him. Any preconceived ideas about this quest had vanished.

Dipping a finger into one of the vessels on the fire, he tested the heat of the tea and was satisfied it was ready. Pouring some of the drink into a shallow bowl, he took it, plus the slab with the salve, and returned to the woman's side. Then he roused her enough to get her to turn over and sit up, her back against one of his arms for support. Her eyes remained closed as he brought the edge of the bowl to her mouth, and as he parted her lips with it enough to pour in a small amount of liquid.

She coughed and grimaced, and her eyes fluttered open. "What *is* that?"

Coyote brought the bowl to his mouth, then, and took a long drink to show her the tea was harmless, hoping she wouldn't resist his efforts. She needed to drink the entire bowl to get results.

"It's *awful*." Her voice was breathless and weak, and her glassy eyes stared into his in an obvious irritation that evolved into confusion.

As he twisted his mouth into a determined line to think what to do to convince her to drink the tea, he watched her reach up with one hand and pinch her two nostrils closed.

"Okay," she said, then closed her eyes and parted her lips.

He smiled, then brought the bowl to her mouth and she swallowed the entire contents.

He set down the bowl and helped her recline back onto the blanket. The activity had tired her greatly and she instantly fell back to sleep. He was glad, because next he planned to bathe her with the creosote wash, and he was certain he would be able to wash her more easily while she slept. Any protests to the bath would only serve to exhaust her even more and thwart his labors completely.

After bringing the other vessel from the fire to the area beside her, he pulled a large square of cloth from his supply bag. His father had given the white man's cloth to him when he was just a young boy. It had been after a trip when his father had been away, working for the *padres* in the valley of the new city. No matter how hard his father had toiled for them—or any white men—instead of money, he'd only been paid in goods and food. The cloth had been part of his payment one season, and he had generously shared it with his people. Coyote fingered the cloth; it was thick, with a good tight weave. He soaked it in the creosote wash and squeezed the excess back out.

First he sponged the woman's face, then her neck and shoulders. He picked up each arm and washed its length, then quickly patted her breasts and stomach, not lingering there. He finished the bath and waited for some of the moisture to leave her skin, then removed her dressings to reapply pulp to her wounds. He added the new jojoba salve to the cut on her head. Finally he re-bandaged her arm and back, and wrapped her body back up in the rabbitskin blanket.

Her pallor seemed already improved, the paleness of her face less offset by her reddened cheeks. She was better. He turned away and set about making a rabbit soup with some dried meat and the fresh cactus pad pieces he'd prepared. He would try to get her to eat if she continued to get better.

As the soup cooked, he leaned against the wall to rest. He hadn't slept in two suns, and weariness overtook him quickly.

When he awoke, he saw two things. His fire had almost burned out, and the woman had again thrown off the blanket. Her cheeks were once again dark scarlet in color, and as he neared her, he could feel the tremendous heat her body radiated. She was much, much worse.

He had been a fool to allow himself sleep. By the looks of it, he had slept for hours and precious time had passed when he should have been watching her more carefully. He clenched his jaw tight, determining his next step.

First he unwrapped her wounds to check them; they seemed the same and maybe a tiny bit better. Then he touched the area close to the cut on her head, and it seemed much less swollen. At least the salve had seemed to help.

She groaned in her sleep, then made soft whimpering sounds. Her breath seemed labored and shallow, and Coyote stared down at her face now pinched from pain. He wrapped her back up in the blanket and returned to kneel by the fire, adding branches and coaxing the embers to flames. He would make a new wash of dried black sage and another batch of tea.

Moving the soup aside, he added ingredients to two freshly filled water vessels. He sat on the ground between the fire and the woman, quieting himself, slowing his breathing, listening within and hoping Grandfather's voice might come to guide him. Many minutes passed, and blurred pictures danced behind the dark of his closed eyelids until finally he was able to calm them. At last a whisper, then a faraway voice came. Grandfather's voice.

*You have done well, my grandson, but the infection is fierce and her spirit is sick; you must try one more thing.*

*What, Grandfather?*

*You must carry out the healing ceremony you saw me do twelve moons ago. Do not be afraid.*

*But only* kuseyaay *do this thing, Grandfather—*

*I will be with you, Coyote, as your hands do this work. And with your medicine and mine, it is only then that this woman may live.*

# *Chapter Five*

*It shall be.*

Coyote opened his eyes. As he struggled to keep his feelings of uncertainty at bay, he took a knife and walked outside the cave to gather the cactus needles he would need for the ceremony.

Returning with many long needles, he held each sharp tip into a flame until it had heated but not burned, then dropped them onto a small scrap of deerskin.

Next he scooped up a few pieces of blackened wood from the edges of the fire to grind in his *'ehpii*. He gripped the pestle in the palm of his hand and thoroughly ground the charcoal against the shallow surface of the granite mortar. Soon he had a small pile of fine black powder.

While he worked, he concentrated on keeping his state of mind steady, an open door so Grandfather could enter and work through him to save the woman. To perform a *kuseyaay* ceremony seemed an impossible task. But he was bound to do it; and do it without question or hesitation.

*"Simiiraay."* It *was* crazy, and his body was filled with anxiety and apprehension.

Tapping the black powder into a bowl, he then placed the deerskin that held the needles on top of the bowl. He reached for the vessel that held the heated black sage wash, and took it and the bowl of powder over to place next to the woman. Then he took two small pieces of cloth from one of his supply bags.

With one of the cloths, he dipped into the vessel of black sage wash and wiped her face and neck, smoothing her hair away from her face to bare her forehead. Then he tucked the rabbitskin blanket tightly around her, binding her arms securely to her sides.

He put the bowl that held the charcoal powder on her chest, and then placed the skin that held the cactus needles beside it. He closed his eyes until he began to hear the song in his mind that Grandfather had sung while performing the healing ceremony he had witnessed twelve moons ago.

Coyote began to mouth the words; then he whispered the words, slowly increasing the volume as he became more sure of himself, and more sure that Grandfather was with him. It was almost as though he could feel the old man sharing his body: Grandfather's hands filling his own hands, his fingers moving within so that when Coyote opened his eyes, he was not surprised to see he already had a cactus needle between his thumb and first finger, ready to begin.

He managed to mentally separate himself, only looking at the expanse of female forehead before him as he began to prick her skin, then take a dab of the black powder and add it to the new wound, blotting with a piece of dry cloth in between.

Back and forth, between needle and powder and forehead he worked, bent over her, close to White Bird's face; working without stopping.

And so it went for a long time. He worked slowly, deliberately, believing he wasn't hurting her, believing Grandfather was with him every moment. A spasm in his lower back broke through the haze, finally, and Coyote sat up straight, blinking away the strange feeling that had consumed him while he'd worked.

*You have done well, grandson.*

Halfway between White Bird's hairline and eyebrows there was now a thin black wavy line, reddened with pricks of dried blood.

*Give her more tea, then she must sleep—as you must sleep also.*

Coyote stared a moment more, then loosened the blanket. Immediately White Bird began to stir, throwing the blanket off, the heat rising from her body to fill the air between them like smoke. He left her for a moment to get the tea, returning to help her sit up.

This time when he held the bowl to her lips, she didn't protest. Instead, she simply parted her lips and drank. As Coyote helped her lie back down, her hand fluttered to her forehead and he grabbed her fingers to stop her from rubbing the fresh tattoo.

"Hurts," she whispered. Her brows pulled together and then her eyes opened a crack.

He held her fingers for a moment, then brought her hand to his chest and opened it so her palm was flat and against his heart. His hope was that she would sense his intent was good, that he'd completed the thing that could heal her, that she was safe with him.

He looked into her eyes—blue eyes like the sky and deep like the water, eyes so unlike his own. She didn't try to speak, only stared at him. Tears escaped from the corners of her eyes, and he watched them make tracks down her cheeks then disappear down the sides of her neck.

He had added to her pain in order to take the pain away. He knew that, but the fact still angered him. *It was crazy.* What had he done?

She cried silently for a few minutes, then her hand became more limp against his chest and her eyes fluttered closed. He put her hand down at her side, then touched her wet cheeks with the back of his fingers. Her cheeks had cooled, and her breathing became deeper and stronger. It was a good sleep.

Returning to the fire, he put the soup back on the rock nearest the heat and stirred it with a wooden spoon. After it had warmed a little, he tasted it. It would be best for him to eat and then sleep, to be ready to prepare more remedies when she awoke.

The soup seemed tasteless to him, but it was good nourishment and he knew he needed to attend to his own body too.

After he finished eating, he tipped the bowl toward the fire to dry the inside, and brought all the other bowls to the fire to do the same. Then he retrieved his dried juncus brush and finished cleaning the dishes, brushing any residue into the fire.

At first he thought he would lean against the wall and sleep as he had done before, but he couldn't get comfortable. He opened his eyes and watched the woman sleeping, her breath even and strong. There was improvement, and he felt great relief. The woman's life connected to his, and the importance of saving her directly affected his own quest, and the outcome of his journey.

"*Simiiraay.*" Though he knew without a doubt the importance of her survival, the craziness of the turn of events for him was still strong and he couldn't completely bury the thought of how absurd it all was. Why would his future depend on a white woman . . . *this* white woman? Why had he dreamt of her? And why did her beauty affect him so deeply? He had never felt so compelled by a woman, not even his former wife. His feelings for White Bird made no sense to him and were deepened by accompanying feelings of guilt, guilt for even considering he could possibly want her.

No, his *body* wanted her. It was his body that had betrayed him. And that he could control. That, he *would* control.

Coyote shook his head and pinched his lips together. He would stay with her until she was well; then he would take her home so his quest could continue, his obligation complete.

Still feeling restless but knowing he needed to sleep, he finally got up and walked over to her, lying next to her so he would be certain to know if she stirred. Finally able to relax, within minutes he was asleep.

Suzanne began to awaken. The first thing she noticed was the foul taste in her mouth, and that her tongue was stuck to the roof of her mouth as though she hadn't had anything to eat or drink in days. She parted her lips to breathe in some air.

She had a tremendous headache, and the inside of her skull pounded painfully with each beat of her heart. Before she opened her eyes, she took inventory of how her entire body felt.

It didn't take long, because pretty much everything hurt. She was afraid to move, guessing she was better off remaining still. Then she sensed a weightiness; her body was covered with something quite heavy. And she felt hot, very hot.

Slowly she opened her eyes a tiny bit, still not

moving. It was dark wherever she was. Then her fingers registered a softness, and she moved her hand against it. *Fur?*

She blinked a few times and waited for her eyes to adjust to the dim light, then lifted her head a little, ignoring the increased pain the movement produced. Lying on the floor next to her was the man she had seen by the pond just before.

What had happened?

Then she began to remember, pictures and thoughts coming to her in flashes. Fever. Swimming. Clothes gone. Shivering cold. *Oh, God.* She had fainted in his arms.

The man lay next to her. He was on his stomach, his long black hair draped over his upper back and shoulder, with one hand on the ground next to his face. In his hand he clutched a knife.

Was she a prisoner? She didn't think so, but her brain was pretty fuzzy. She tried hard to remember what had happened after she'd fainted, but nothing came to her, and thinking was as painful as lifting her head had been.

Dropping her head back onto the fur, she closed her eyes to rest, still trying to use logic to reach a conclusion that made sense.

But nothing made sense.

He would have harmed her already if that was his intent, she reasoned. And he hadn't. She had a vague sense that he had helped her; he had covered her up at least. Then she remembered his eyes: black, intense eyes. Eyes that hadn't revealed danger, but instead, reassurance.

No, she wasn't a prisoner. She was certain he had tried to help her.

The realization was comforting, and she felt her body grow heavy again with fatigue. Just the little bit of movement and thinking had taken a toll. She let herself drift back to sleep.

The next time Suzanne woke, the light in the cave was bright. She hadn't moved; she was still on her stomach facing where the man had been lying. When she opened her eyes completely, though, he wasn't there at all. Instead, there was a shallow wooden bowl on the floor.

She reached out her hand and pulled the bowl close, then tipped it a little to see inside. Liquid. *Water*? Dipping a finger into the liquid she brought it first to her nose, then her tongue. Definitely water.

When she brought the bowl to her lips, at first she forced herself to take only a few sips. Once she was sure it was staying down, she continued to sip, then waited, then sipped a little more. The moisture was soothing to her tongue and throat, and already seemed to be lessening the light-headedness she felt—a symptom of her obvious dehydration. How long had she been asleep?

Then she noticed a bit of what looked like beef jerky on a scrap of deerskin. Pulling it to her, she picked a piece up and sniffed. It had a gamy smell, but her growling stomach approved. She put some in her mouth, letting her saliva soften it before she began to chew. Not beef, she was pretty sure, but tasty enough. She chewed thoroughly, then swallowed, then continued until she had eaten all the pieces.

The movement exhausted her and as soon as she put her head back down she dozed off. The next time she awakened, the light was growing dim again. The fur blanket was still under her, but over her was a thin, soft piece of buckskin that felt wonderful and cool against her skin. She tried to shove away the embarrassing thought that she was still quite naked under the cover *and* that her rescuer had obviously been caring for her for a while, dressing her wounds and, by the looks of how clean she was, washing away any dried blood or dirt. She looked around, hoping she'd see her clothes folded in a neat little pile nearby.

Not a sign of them.

But what she did see was another bowl of water and more bits of dried meat. She pushed herself up to a sitting position, then wrapped the deerskin blanket around her chest like a bath towel, tucking in the end securely before she reached for the bowl of water.

As she drank and ate, she looked more closely at her surroundings. Some of her caretaker's things were stacked against the walls and scattered about: a primitive looking bow leaned against the wall near her, plus a leather quiver filled with arrows. Various containers were on the opposite side; some bags made of deerskin, woven baskets, carved wooden bowls, clay pots, and a few utensils and crude tools. There was a low fire near the entrance of the cave, and on some flat rocks at one edge of the fire was a steaming pot of something. *Dinner?* Her stomach rumbled hopefully.

Then the light was blocked for an instant, and when she blinked, she realized she had company. He was back. As the man stepped into the cave carrying an armload of wood, he didn't look at her, but proceeded to stack the wood in a pile. Then he added a few pieces to the fire until flames licked at the simmering pot.

He looked the same as she thought she remembered . . . the same as when she'd seen him the first time, just before she'd fainted, and the same as when she'd woken up and he was lying next to her. He had amazingly long black hair, well past his shoulders; dark eyes, a muscular chest and legs, and was wearing only a simple breechcloth. He looked like something from a living museum display or a reenactors group.

Perhaps he was one of those survivalists, or maybe he was into really primitive camping, she reasoned. He certainly looked the part, either way.

She watched as he reached for a wooden spoon and stirred the contents of the clay pot, then brought a spoonful out to taste. As the spoon almost reached his lips, his gaze finally rose and met hers. He stared, his eyes widening as if he were surprised—no, more like he was examining her. Then his gaze dropped to the empty water bowl on the ground beside her, then the scrap of deerskin devoid of meat. The look on his face evolved into one of satisfaction, then relief. And finally, his expression worked itself into a smile as he once again met her stare.

Without hesitation, Suzanne smiled back. "Thank you." He tipped his head slightly to the side at the sound of her words. "You don't understand me, do you?" She frowned, then pointed at the water bowl and empty piece of deerskin, then brought her fingertips to her lips and made chewing motions before sighing dramatically and rubbing her stomach.

His left eyebrow rose a fraction; then he nodded and pointed to the simmering pot.

"Whatever it is," she said, "I'd love some." She pointed a finger at the pot and nodded. He motioned for her to stay where she was, then dipped a small bowl into the pot and brought it and the spoon to her.

She took the spoon and bowl from him and brought it close to her face, breathed in the aroma, then dipped the spoon in for a taste while he got himself a bowlful. It wasn't a soup at all, which is what she'd guessed. It was more like a cornmeal mush, with bits of some kind of roasted meat in it. The taste was somewhat bland, but the food was hot and hearty, and she knew it would provide much needed energy. Her body craved carbs and protein.

She chewed methodically, watching her caretaker as he also ate. Occasionally he looked up at her as he poked at the fire, scooting coals around—she guessed he was banking it for the night. Then he pointed at her bowl, then the pot, and she assumed he was asking her if she wanted more.

"No, I don't think I better eat any more right now." She shook her head, then started to get up to bring him the bowl. He watched her and frowned.

"I'm fine," she said as she steadied herself with one hand against the wall. "A little dizzy, but not too bad."

What she really needed to do was go outside and relieve her full bladder and she was determined to make the trip on her own. Tiny dark stars floated in front of her eyes, created from her moving to a standing position after having been lying down for so long. She paused until she thought she would be able to walk without faltering.

She focused on his face and tried to maintain an expression of confidence. His frown deepened as she stumbled a little walking toward him, and he started to get up.

"Oh, no. *You* stay *here*. I've got to go outside to . . ." What was she supposed to say? That her bladder was about to burst and she needed to find a nice bush, and fast? She stared at him while she considered how to make him stay put and assure him she was fine and that she'd be right back.

Before she could think of how she might hand-signal *bathroom*, he nodded determinedly and exchanged the bowl she was still carrying for a stick that she could use to brace herself.

"Okay." She walked slowly out of the cave, and a small distance away she squatted, grateful he had thought to give her the walking stick. Her legs were rubbery and she was still a little light-headed; she'd needed the extra support to walk the short distance and to lean on so she could more easily get up from her crouched position.

When she finished, she made her way back toward the pond. The light had faded completely and the temperature dropped several degrees. While she walked, she again looked for anything that might look more familiar. *No*, she corrected herself, more *modern*. It was the same thought she'd had when she'd trekked back and forth, looking for the familiar trail after the earthquake. The path had been there, sort of, but it had seemed different. No real signs of civilization were anywhere along the trail.

So, what had happened? All signs of the civilized world had just vanished into thin air after the earthquake? It was either that or somehow she was *before* all the missing things had been built.

The thought came, unbidden and unwanted. *Another time.* A time before . . . before what?

Or, maybe she was dreaming—a lovely, adventurous dream with a built-in hero to take care of her. Could she be experiencing her dreamworld, but in a more conscious state of mind? It sort of made a little sense, she rationalized, looking for any possible truth. Her surroundings were definitely familiar to her if she measured them against her dreamworld and not against the modern world.

Could a person dream, and know she was dreaming?

Suzanne groaned, her brain suddenly as weary as her body. She needed to get back to the cave and lie down, but she couldn't ignore the nagging hope that at least some of her questions might be answered by the light of day. After some rest, she'd be able to think more clearly. She was counting on it.

When she stooped to enter the cave, she saw the fire was reduced to glowing embers, and the man had already bedded down. His back faced her and she could hear his soft, steady breathing.

With her gaze fixed on him, she lowered herself onto the fur blanket, then unwrapped the deerskin from around herself, quickly shook it out, and crawled under it. She pulled the cover up to her neck, then tucked it snugly in her armpits with each arm firmly at her sides.

Forcing her eyes closed, she listened to her caretaker's breathing, and then to the same night sounds that had surrounded her that first night she'd spent in the cave alone.

The overwhelming thought, which became a pre-sleep mantra, was that for the first time, every part of her being agreed it was good *not* to be alone. And if she was dreaming, fine. This was her Indian dream man. And if she wasn't dreaming, then he could be a simple rescuer. He obviously knew what he was doing. True, there was a bit of a language barrier, but they'd managed so far.

Tomorrow, if she was strong enough, maybe she would take him to the trailhead, and they could go together toward the campground to see if anything had changed.

# Chapter Six

When Suzanne opened her eyes again, the light in the cave had changed and she figured she had slept through the night and well into the next day. From head to toe she felt much better, and easily sat up and wrapped the deerskin around her body while she looked around.

She was alone; a bowl of water and a bowl of mush sat on the ground next to her. First she drank the water, then carefully she stood to go outside to eat. Her legs were steady under her, and she ignored the walking stick that still leaned against the wall.

Her pain had all but disappeared and she was surprised. Once during the night she'd awakened from the throb of a headache, but had drifted back to sleep after only a short while. She'd had a sense her caretaker had checked on her, a vague memory of the feel of his hand on her cheeks, and then of drinking something. Not much else.

Now she felt almost normal. As she ducked her head to step out of the cave, she saw the man walking toward her, his arms loaded with firewood. His dark eyes widened a little, then he glared and pointed a finger and tipped his head toward a rock next to the pond.

"Okay, okay—I just needed a change of scenery. I'm fine. I feel great." She dropped down anyway, to sit on the flat stone next to the water, tucking the deerskin securely under her legs.

He pointed to the bowl in her hands and said, "*Kesaaw.*"

She watched as he took the branches into the cave and dropped them just inside, then came back outside and stared at her.

"Is that what this is . . . *kesaaw?*" She repeated the word, pointed at the contents of the bowl and smiled. "Mmmmmm . . . it's good. *Kesaaw.*" She hoped he understood her gratitude, even though the gruel was cold, sticky, and difficult to swallow.

He studied her; then he walked closer so he could point inside the bowl. "*Shawii.*"

Suzanne stared down at the bowl. *Shawii?* She knew that word . . .

After a few minutes, she finally remembered why. She'd first heard it on a guided hike she and her students had taken at the San Dieguito River Park in the northern part of the county. Heather had been their guide, an extremely knowledgeable woman who studied the history of the Native American people of the area. The

*Kumeyaay* were hunters and gatherers—mostly gatherers, she'd explained as she'd pointed out a few examples of native plants they would have used for food or medicine. It had been fascinating, Suzanne remembered, and tied in well with the class she herself taught on native plants and their uses. It had been a perfect field trip, and she'd added it to her own curriculum.

Heather always ended the hike at the replica of a *Kumeyaay* kitchen she and other park volunteers had created: a configuration of rocks that had basins and grooves in the surfaces similar to what *Kumeyaay* women would have used to grind acorns and other foods.

*Shawii* was the *Kumeyaay* word for acorn mush.

"*Shawii*," she said, looking back at him. "It's good, thank you. Thank you for feeding me so well." He seemed pleased—at least his expression softened as he watched her eat, remaining where he was until she'd forced down the last bite.

He nodded at her empty bowl, then took it from her to clean. While he was inside the cave, she used his absence to walk a bit and look for a private spot to relieve herself.

When she got back to the pond, she sat on the stone again instead of going inside the cave to join him. When she ducked her head enough to peek inside the mouth of the cave, she could see he was busy banking the fire again for the night.

She remained where she was—craving the

fresh air and, more importantly, the time to think.

Night fell as she found herself simply staring into the water, finally settling on the idea of stepping into the pond to bathe. She turned toward the cave and, satisfied he was still occupied, unwrapped her deerskin. Stretching out her arms to hold it out behind her, shielding her body from his view, she walked into the water, lifting the deerskin up and away from her. When most of her body was submerged, she gathered the wrap and carefully draped it over a branch that hung out over the water, but well within her reach so she could retrieve it before she got out.

He'd probably soon bed down for the night, and she wasn't the least bit sleepy. She realized she felt really alert for the first time since the earthquake, and was in much better shape to try to sort out her thoughts about what had happened to her.

Pushing herself down completely into the water she submerged her head, then tried to pull her fingers through her hair to untangle it. When she came up for air, she already felt more refreshed and clean. With one arm reaching back over her shoulder, she gently felt for the deep wound she knew was there. It had scabbed over and didn't feel nearly as tender. Then she checked her head wound; it, too, was barely swollen, and just a tiny bit sore. The scrape on her arm was in even better shape. Whatever he'd done to treat her had worked miracles.

She swam slowly from one end of the pond to the other, and back again. Stretching out her arms and legs, she loosened the stiff joints as she breast-stroked through the water; all the while keeping an eye out for the man.

Who was he? Had she discovered a hermit who'd evaded modern men and modern ways for the last hundred years? Maybe he was part of some hidden tribe? Or, maybe he was like that woman from San Nicholas Island, alone for almost twenty years and living a primitive lifestyle while the rest of the world rode on the wave of progress.

It didn't quite ring true, but she wasn't sure why. This was too populated an area, maybe. Too many tourists and rock hounds and hikers were about; it was too hard to avoid being noticed by *someone*. Park rangers, at the very least, would have seen him or seen signs of him.

He seemed so comfortable at the oasis, too. As though he had camped here many times. And it would have been impossible for him to go unnoticed with the thousands of people who visited the campground throughout the year.

Her head began to throb from the effort of pulling together strings of logical explanations and then, one by one, refuting each. Again she submerged her head and tried to smooth out her long hair. This time, when she came up for air and wiped her eyes, the man was sitting on the flat stone at the water's edge.

His gaze caught hers, and he pointed to his

back and touched the same spot where the wound was on her back. Then he pointed at her.

She nodded. "It's fine. You did a great job, by the way. I don't remember much. I know I had a high fever . . . and I remember something awful-tasting that you kept making me drink." She cupped her hands and brought them to her lips as if to drink, then made a sour face.

The man laughed softly, then nodded.

Well, at least they were communicating. She swam a little closer to him, chuckling. "You do look like an honest-to-goodness real hero, you know. Not exactly a knight in shining armor—but close enough. My friend Robin would call you drop-dead gorgeous, and insist that you'd be perfect for me."

His expression remained unchanged, though he seemed to be listening intently.

"And my wounds are all but healed. Maybe you're a medicine man, huh?"

He looked toward the piece of deerskin she'd hung on the branch, then looked at her.

"Hey, don't even think about taking off with my one and only outfit." She still wondered what had happened to her clothes; too many things seemed to have simply vanished into thin air.

Then the man stood and began undoing his loincloth.

"Oh, jeez!" Suzanne sank fully into the water just as he pulled the bit of deerskin from his body. From under the surface she heard a splash, and she felt the surge his dive produced.

She pulled her head out of the water and saw him swimming toward the far end of the pond, his black hair streaming behind him. He disappeared below the surface and brought his head out of the water a few yards away from her.

He rubbed his face and chest, loosening any grime that might be there, then began to swim back toward the rock by the shoreline.

She turned away just as the water dipped below his waist and he stepped out.

"You go ahead," she said, then turned around to peek if he had dressed. He had, and he was standing on the shoreline as though he were waiting for her.

"I think I'll stay for a while and soak. I'm fine, really." Her gaze met his, and she watched his eyes narrow a bit, perhaps worried about her judgment.

"Honest. Just a few more minutes and I'll come in. I want to try to untangle my hair." She pulled her hair over her shoulders in front and started untangling the blond waves, glancing up at him to see if he understood her.

He nodded, then patted his chest and pointed into the cave.

"Right. You go on in and I promise I won't be long."

He turned and ducked to enter the cave.

She concentrated on untangling her hair, bringing a piece to her face to examine and to smell. Not too bad, but perhaps tomorrow she

could convince him to take her for a walk—
maybe to look for the trail, and while they were
out, she could look for a Mojave yucca. She'd
seen pictures of how the local Indians used
scrapings from its root to make suds for soap to
clean the skin and hair; she could probably figure out how to do it.

Using her fingernails, she parted out a triangle
on top of her head, divided the long strands into
three, and began French-braiding until her hair
was in a thick plait down the back of her head,
ending at the nape of her neck. She continued
until she had braided the full length.

Her arms ached by the time she'd finished, but
her patience was rewarded with a feeling she
probably looked much more neat and present-
able.

Wading through the shallow water, she made
her way toward her wrap, and carefully retrieved it from the branch. Keeping her eyes on
the mouth of the cave, she held the deerskin in
front of her as she waded out of the water, dripping for a few minutes while she held the skin
in front of her like a curtain. Finally satisfied she
had air-dried as much as possible, she wrapped
herself in the skin and sat on the rock.

She followed the edge of the deerskin until she
found where she'd noticed a tear. If she could
pull a thin piece off, it would be perfect to tie
the end of her braid. The edge with the tear
seemed thin enough to pull on, and soon she had
a leather string of deerskin. She chewed the end

that was still attached until it was free, then wrapped it around the end of her braid and tied it in a square knot.

She felt tidy and groomed for the first time in days. With one last look at the night sky, she went into the cave to bed down.

"This is good stuff." Suzanne sat on her fur blanket while her caretaker sat on the other side of the fire watching her. That morning he had again prepared *shawii*, and had also offered her bits of some kind of roasted meat that had a strong fishy taste, but she found if she dipped it in the mush, it was tolerable.

She hadn't heard him get up, and she'd slept in. Even though she knew it was still quite early, when her eyes blinked open the fire had already been stoked and her meal was waiting for her.

"I could get used to this service. You're spoiling me, you know."

He met her gaze silently.

When she was finished eating, instead of handing him her bowl, she leaned onto her knees and reached for the brush she had seen him use to clean out the dishes. It was about four inches long, with course bristles of fiber whose curved ends had hook-like tips. She examined the brush carefully, then recognized it as the root of a soaproot plant. It was perfect.

She glanced toward her caretaker as she worked, and his eyes followed her every move. "Is this right?"

He dropped his chin a little in a curt nod, then reached for the brush and bowl when she extended them to him.

He turned away, then reached for his bow and quiver of arrows.

"Hey, where are you going?" Scrambling to her feet, Suzanne stepped closer to him.

He turned and pointed at her and then to the floor.

"But I don't want to stay here," she said. "Take me with you." She pointed to herself, then to him, and toward the mouth of the cave.

He shook his head no, and his eyebrows pulled together in a deep frown.

"I'm fine. I really want to go." She made walking motions in the air with two fingers, then took the end of her braid and put it to her nose. She made a face. "I need to find a yucca . . . a plant that I can make soap from." She concentrated, searching for a way to make him understand soap. First she pantomimed shampooing her hair, then rubbed her arms and legs, finally pointing toward the water.

His face grew even more serious as he watched her, and again he pointed to her and then to the ground. As though dismissing both her and her request, he turned away and left the cave before she could speak again.

"Fine, I'll just go by myself." As she waited for him to get out of sight, she looked around outside the cave for something she might dig with, finally finding a stick made of some kind of sturdy hardwood. It would be perfect to help her get at the root of any plant.

A welcome feeling of independence and confidence filled her as she grabbed the stick and left the cave. It felt good to have a goal, a purpose. Today she'd make soap and maybe tomorrow she'd make him understand she wanted him to take her to find the trail to the campground. If he wouldn't, she'd simply go by herself.

She'd walked several minutes in a new direction away from the oasis, careful to stay on what looked like at least a primitive walking path, watchful for any sharp rocks or sticks that might injure her bare feet. Fairly quickly she located a small cluster of yuccas; their yellow-green bayonet-like leaves were about two feet long, and formed a spiny puffball at the top of gray-brown trunks. Dried leaves hung downward along the trunk forming a dense skirt.

After deciding which plant was the smallest and in the best position along the perimeter of the grouping, she began to dig with the stick at the base of the trunk. When she'd uncovered the root, she chipped away at it until she had several large chunks that would be perfect to take shavings from, and then replaced the displaced sandy soil. If she couldn't find his knife back at the cave, she'd have to try to make him understand she'd need to borrow one to scrape the root and make shavings that, mixed with water, would create suds.

The work had exhausted her, and the feeling

of light-headedness returned with a vengeance, accompanied by an unexpected wave of nausea. She fell to her knees before they buckled, panic rushing through her. She concentrated on gathering her wits, telling herself to remain calm and to breathe deep breaths. What had she been thinking? She hadn't brought any water, her head was uncovered and exposed to the now blazing sun, and her newfound strength had been completely expended. It was clear to her that she couldn't make it back to the cave in her current condition.

*Think . . .* She looked around through blurred vision, and finally made the decision to crawl toward a nearby boulder. Near its base was a large indentation; if she curled up into it, the space would at least offer some shade. The ground should be cooler, and she'd be out of the direct sunlight; she could rest there until she had the strength to get herself back to camp.

He'd been right. It was too soon for her to have walked into the morning heat, and especially to have exerted herself with such a physical task. And she knew better—knew better than to not take the time to consider the consequences of placing herself in such a vulnerable position. The desert was a harsh environment, and not one to be taken for granted.

She wriggled into the space, drawing her knees up to her chin. It was cooler there, and she felt safer. Her eyes closed, obliterating the blurred scene in front of her. She would rest, just for a few minutes, just until her strength returned.

Coyote's hunt was unsuccessful, and he knew the anger he'd felt when he'd left White Bird in the morning had affected his power to stalk the woodrat. There would be no fresh meat for dinner, and even the sun had punished him during his efforts. The beginning of the day had been hotter than it had been in weeks, with no wind to cool him while he waited for woodrat to show himself.

By noon he had given up. He would return empty-handed except for the green yucca leaves he'd gathered to weave a pair of sandals for the woman. If she continued to insist on leaving the cave to do any amount of walking, her tender feet would need their protection.

As he focused on the path ahead, he almost missed her. Tucked into a crevice at the base of a rock, he saw her body curled into a ball, her mouth open and panting.

She had either followed him or perhaps gone for a walk and gotten lost; it didn't matter. He approached her, placed his quiver and bow on the ground, then dropped to one knee beside her.

" '*Aashaa nemeshap*." He whispered her name as he nudged her shoulder, trying to rouse her.

"What?" Her voice was weak, and she sounded frightened.

When her eyes fluttered open, they were

glassy with sickness from the heat. She had walked a long way from the cave and he saw no water vessel nearby. He should have been more clear with her, worked harder to convince her she should stay at the camp until she had healed completely, that she shouldn't be venturing far when she was alone.

She was a stubborn woman, and it would be good for him to keep that in mind. In the future, he would need to be much more stern with her. Then he pulled her toward him so he could put her in a position to lift her. After he'd rolled her away from the rock, he saw chunks of yucca root fall from her hands.

" *'Emaa,*" he said as he tucked a piece of root into the waist of his breechcloth. He hadn't really believed she would hunt for the yucca root on her own. It was a good lesson; next time he would take her talk more seriously.

She moaned as he scooped her up and draped her over his shoulder. Then he grabbed his bow and quiver, and trotted down the path toward the cave hoping he had found her in time.

# *Chapter Seven*

It was late in the afternoon and Suzanne sat on the edge of the pond, her knees drawn up close to her chest and her chin resting on her crossed arms. Her memory of what had happened was fuzzy; she remembered going out in the morning to look for the yucca root and how she'd crawled under the boulder to rest, but not much else. She assumed he must have found her on his way back from hunting. Always her rescuer.

She had awakened from a long nap—in a foul mood—a blend of anger, frustration, and depression. Her patience was gone, and she wanted answers. She *needed* answers.

When she sensed she wasn't alone, she lifted her head to see him staring at her, and though his eyes brimmed with concern, his mouth was set in a stern line. He tried to hand her a bowl of something, but she turned away. She had no appetite, and just the thought of food brought back the nausea she'd felt earlier.

"Go away. I'm depressed and mad. I just want to know what the hell has happened to me, where the hell I am and who the hell *you* are! Leave me alone so I can think about my options, here. Jeez—what am I supposed to do? There has to be a way to get myself out of here."

She glanced at him, but he hadn't moved an inch.

"Go *away*." She gestured toward the cave. "I know you're doing the best you can, but I'm sick of trying to be cheerful and grateful about it. You're like some good guy in a comic book— always there to take care of me and save me. But, the thing is, what I want you don't have. And what I want are some answers that make sense."

She turned away from him, staring at the dark water of the pool. A moment later she felt his body close to hers as he joined her on the rock, sitting close enough that she could feel the warmth radiating from his skin. Then she felt the gentle touch of his hand on her shoulder— the tenderness of it brought tears to her eyes. She sniffed them back, determined not to cry in front of him.

"Please go away. I'm not usually this emotional, you know. I'm the one who always has a plan. Always organized. Always in control. Never needing anyone's help—or wanting it." One hot tear escaped and slid down her cheek. "*Dammit*. Stop being so *nice* to me—it just makes it worse. And tomorrow, whether you like it or not, I'm taking another look at the trail back to the campground . . . with or without you. I've got to see if anything has changed."

" *'Aashaa nemeshap.*"

His fingertips were now on her chin, forcing her to look at him. He pointed at her and repeated the words, then pointed at himself and said, "*Hattepaa.*"

"I don't understand you." She jerked free from his grasp.

This time, he took one of her hands and placed it on his chest, just over his heart. "*Hattepaa.*" He nodded curtly toward her, and waited.

"*Hattepaa,*" she whispered back to him, her heart pounding. Her gaze shifted from his chest to his lips, and finally to his dark eyes. As she stared into them she knew if circumstances were very different she could easily get lost in their liquid blackness. "You have such kind eyes, you know. Even when you're trying to be strict with me or serious, your eyes are a dead giveaway. *GQ* would be after those eyes; you'd have a modeling career in LA or New York. Robin would be right in calling you drop-dead gorgeous."

Her voice trailed off as he took her hand and moved it to her chest, resting it over her heart.

"*Aashaa nemeshap.*" He said the words slowly, then pulled his own hand away and nodded at her, indicating for her to repeat them.

"What does it mean? I get it that you want to call me that, but—"

He interrupted her with a raised finger, and

she watched as he pinched his eyes closed as though he were concentrating with all his effort.

Then his lips parted as they began to form a word. "Buh ... buh ... bird. Bird. White Bird."

She stared at him and felt her jaw drop, her mouth now gaping open. "You speak *English*?" Anger and embarrassment erupted inside her, and she groaned. Had he understood everything she'd been saying?

His eyes snapped opened and then grew wide to reveal his confusion.

"Do ... you ... speak ... *English*?" She said the words slowly, and emphasized each word through clenched jaws.

He nodded slowly. "Little."

She felt the blaze in her cheeks and looked away; she should be happy, but she felt betrayed instead. Why had he hidden it all this time?

"*Hattepaa* ... Coyote." His voice was strong; he was obviously pleased with himself.

It changed everything.

She brought her hands up to cover her eyes, and then groaned again. *Jeez, what did I just say? All that stuff about him and his gorgeous eyes, and him being good-looking and ... okay, be logical for a minute. This is a good thing. Increased communication. Conversation, even. And it'll be easier to explain what happened to me and to get him to take me up the trail in the morning.*

She dropped her hands back to her lap and turned toward him, a forced smile on her face. "Okay, let's start over." She brought her hand to her chest and said, "Suzanne. That's my English name. Su-zanne."

He frowned and repeated the word slowly, though it sounded more like *soSAHN*.

"Are you *Kumeyaay*? *Diegueño*? *Luiseño*?"

His brows knit together as though he were angered by her question. "Padre say *Diegueño*. My people *Kumeyaay*." He accentuated the word, and his eyes narrowed as if to measure her response.

"Of course. *Kumeyaay*. I meant no offense. So," she continued, "will you take me to the trail?" She stopped to think how she was going to explain exactly what she wanted. Spinning around on the rock, she took a stick and began to sketch a crude representation in the dirt.

"Okay, here's the pond and the cave. We're here." She pointed at him and then herself, and finally made a sweep of her arm to indicate their surroundings.

Coyote nodded, first pointing at the mouth of the cave, then the water next to them, and finally at her drawing.

"Perfect." He understood. She felt a surge of energy from the unexpected shift in events, and she was optimistic answers would be forthcoming. Progress was a wonderful thing.

She continued to draw a long line extending from the oasis to depict the trail, drawing mountains made of inverted Vs to give him a clue of the foothills that surrounded the campground.

He stared at her drawing and nodded. Then

he held up a finger, got up and disappeared into the cave. He was back in a moment with a pair of crudely woven sandals.

"Are those for me?"

He reached for one of her feet and held the bottom of a sandal against it to check the size.

"Looks like a good fit. Did you make these?"

He sat beside her and helped her try them on.

Pointing at the sandals she said, "Shoes. These are shoes."

"Shoes." He nodded, as though perhaps remembering the word.

She hadn't really considered the danger in walking the trail barefoot, but he obviously had. "Thank you. You think we could go now instead of in the morning?"

His face registered his immediate displeasure.

"It's not that late." She looked at the sky and guessed they had a good four hours until dusk.

"Better in morning."

"But I really want to go *now*—I've got shoes, thanks to you, and I feel fine. Look, I'll even eat first." She picked up the bowl of mush he'd brought out and began to eat, using the small shell that was sitting in the bowl as a spoon.

Even though his face darkened and his mouth almost grimaced, she could see in his eyes that he would give in to her request.

He pointed to the bowl and gave her a nod, then got up and walked away.

\* \* \*

Coyote entered the cave and grabbed his bow and quiver, a knife, and a water gourd. He understood White Bird wanted to go down the trail away from the pond, but he had no clear idea how far she meant to go.

He saw the strength of her determination and didn't think he could fight it. And besides, there he might find a clue about where her home was, or perhaps the trail would lead to where her people were.

Much had changed in an instant. Speaking the white man's English had felt strange, but not wrong—at least in this situation. It was one of the only useful things his father had taught him. Each time he'd returned from his many trips away, the man had told him of the riches of the white man's world and shared what he'd learned of their language. Learning the words and their meaning had indeed been useful in protecting himself from the evils of the white man.

He'd been surprised how much he'd understood of White Bird's language and how easily the words had just now formed on his lips. He would need to try to get her to slow down, though, so he could relearn words and practice them.

By the time he returned outside, she had rinsed the bowl and seemed eager to leave. He barely glanced at her as he headed toward the trail.

* * *

Suzanne easily kept up with Coyote's steady pace now that her feet were protected with the homemade sandals. She didn't take much notice of the surroundings, but instead concentrated on trying to match his stride, quickly getting used to the flat soles and the feel of the woven yucca leaves.

When she did glance around, she noticed there still were no mile markers or plant signs. And the rubble still covered the path so thickly in spots that she was glad he knew where they were going, because to her the trail seemed to disappear every few yards.

Landmarks appeared that seemed somewhat familiar, but she had a feeling they were familiar because of the many times she'd trekked back toward the campground the evening of the earthquake. She was losing hope with every step, but she was still glad to be walking toward what *might* be.

"Wait! This is it!" She scooted around him to run ahead into the clearing, then stopped in her tracks.

"Home?" he asked when he caught up with her.

"It's still not right." She shook her head, her eyes searching the expanse in front of them. There were no signs of the world she'd left behind.

"Go more?"

"I don't think so." She sighed. "It's all just . . .

*gone.* I don't know how to explain it to you—"

"Slow," he said, interrupting her.

She felt the touch of his fingertips on her forearm. Again, unwanted tears formed. "Give me a minute." Tipping her head back a little so the tears found a pathway down her throat instead of her cheeks, she waited. What was she supposed to say—that the world she knew had simply vanished?

"Show me," he said, and held out a stick.

She took it and sat on a rock. "This trail," she said, pointing at the path, "is different now. *My* trail came from a campground . . . a place with people and buildings." She pointed to the space where the restrooms should be. "Right there, should be a building."

She drew in the dirt, sketching out the bathroom and shower building. Then she pointed toward the area where her tent had been.

"Over there, was my tent and my car." She drew both, then looked at him.

His brow furrowed and he pointed at the tent in the drawing. "Home." Then he pointed at the car and shook his head. "Wagon? You have horse?"

She stared at him. If he had been hidden away for years, it certainly was possible he'd never seen a car, she thought, but her gut was telling her it was more than that. It was more like he didn't know what a car *was*.

"Go now. Night come soon." He returned her stare, his face neutral.

She looked once more at the landscape that surrounded them, then nodded in agreement.

Immediately he turned and began walking away from the scene.

The trip back to the cave was a silent one, and she pushed away all thought. It was too frustrating to believe they'd come all this way to simply see the same scene, the scene she'd so been wishing would be different this time.

Keeping her focus on the path, she glanced up every few minutes to see her caretaker's muscular back, his long hair bouncing as he jumped over a rock or branch in the trail. Occasionally he'd turn to look over his shoulder at her, but quickly spin away before she could read his face.

He must think she was crazy. And maybe a part of her was. At that moment, all she could think about was getting back to the cave and going to sleep. Maybe in her dreams there would be images of home, or perhaps there would be a message, some explanation she could hold on to.

After he was certain White Bird was asleep, Coyote rose from his bed without a sound and left the cave. He stood next to the pond and looked into the dark water, finally closing his eyes as he quieted himself.

*Grandfather?*

*I am here, Coyote.*

*White Bird asked me to take her up the path that travels away from the water and to the great clearing.*

*And what did you find there?*

114

*Space. Sky. Sadness. She is healed, Grandfather, and she wants to go home.*

*The time is not right, Coyote, for her to leave. You must still care for her, protect her. And, you must learn from her.*

*I am remembering the white man's English my father taught me.*

*That is good. Speak White Bird's language. Listen to her dreams and you will begin to understand.*

Coyote felt Grandfather's spirit leave his mind just as the sharp call of the night owl filled the air. He dropped to sit on the flat rock by the water.

He'd hoped White Bird's people would be waiting where she'd thought, hoped he could deliver her to safety and continue with his own quest. Now there would be more delays; more precious time would pass until he could go ahead with his own plans.

But he needed to work harder to control his irritation; this was clear. And Grandfather's message was clear as well. Though something inside him cringed at speaking her language, he admitted he was intrigued by what the white woman might teach him.

As a young man he'd been curious and had gone with his father a few times to work on ranches where settlers had moved; all were places where his own people had once lived. When they'd arrived, the white men had simply begun building their houses, then hired the Indians to work on the land.

Janet Wellington

During his many times away, his father had managed to learn their language well, though he seldom spoke in front of the white men. Children, sometimes, tried to teach their lessons to him. He had told Coyote many times that the children started out kind and playful, but soon became mean and distrustful.

Coyote tried to picture White Bird on a rancheria or living in one of the towns that prospered in the valley close to the mission. He tried to imagine her living in one of the areas from which his own people had been evicted, pushed farther away from the river because that was their only choice.

He couldn't picture her there. She didn't belong there, somehow. But he couldn't come up with any real reason why she didn't.

"What are you doing out here?"

The sound of her voice startled him, surprised him that he hadn't heard her footsteps.

She repeated her question as he stared at her, still searching for the right word in English. Then he tipped his head to one side and tapped it with one finger. "*Iichaa*."

She matched his tipped head, and smiled. "Thinking?"

"Of many moons ago."

"Oh, *remembering*. Thinking about long ago is remembering."

Her face grew brighter in the moonlight, pleased she had found his word for him. He returned her smile. "What you doing here?" he asked.

Her smile grew until she finally laughed, and it was a sound that made him believe her heart, too, had begun to heal.

"Well, I was asleep and dreaming. Then I woke up and you were gone. I was confused, and so I came out to find you."

"*Hemach.*"

"What?"

"Dream," he explained. "Dream good?"

"Can I sit with you?" She pointed to the rock.

He nodded and slid over to make room for her. "Tell me?" he asked, then watched her eyes darken and her brows pull together in a frown, her face filled with conflicting emotions.

"I'll try." Her voice came out in a whisper. "When I was a girl, my dreams were about . . . here, mostly."

She had turned her face toward the water, and it was difficult to read her emotions, but he sensed her joy had dissipated or at least changed into something else. He concentrated, listening carefully as she began to speak, amazed he recalled so much of her language.

"I know this place." She extended her arms, indicating the pond and the trees and the surrounding rocks. "To me, this is Borrego Palm Canyon." She said the words slowly and turned to look at him; her gaze met his as if to see if he understood. Then she reached beside herself to scoop up a handful of the sand and fine rock. "I love the desert," she explained, and she let the sand slip from her fingers and back to the ground.

He nodded, suddenly remembering the word. He pointed at the ground, shook his head and corrected her. "*Mes-haraay.*" Then he pointed to the more general area, pointing at the plants and rocks and ground. " '*Emtaar.* Desert. My people come here for good plants."

"In my dreams—when I was a girl and even now—I am *here*. And there is a boy, and sometimes an old man in my dreams. I don't remember very much, but it's a good place, always a good dream. I am happy there, happier there than anywhere."

She leaned forward to dip her cupped hand into the pond and splashed water on her face.

He wasn't certain if talking about her dreams had made her upset, or if she simply sought relief from the warm night. The air had stilled after darkness had come, and it felt heavy, as though the heat of the day still lingered. "Tell me dream . . . *this* night."

Her lips spread into a thin line before she answered. "Tonight, I dreamed of my home. It's very different there—loud, big, everything is so . . . fast. There are many buildings there and many, many people."

"*Kumeyaay?*"

"Your people all live on reservations," she replied, her voice growing soft.

He nodded. He had heard of the idea of keeping his people in one spot. His own people had chosen to move toward the mountains as the valley and coast became more and more populated; they'd kept moving in order to avoid the restrictions they saw coming. The whites talked about setting aside some land for them, but not good land. They had repeatedly ignored their own treaties and pushed his people farther and farther into the rocks and hills.

"In my home," she continued, "there are giant buildings as tall as these palms, as tall as many palms end to end." She pointed to the tops of the trees, then to the surrounding cliffs. "Some higher even than those rocks."

He watched as she pointed toward the highest cliffs, then shook his head. "I have been to the valley. I see your villages. *Not* higher than many trees or rocks. Padres are there. Kumeyaay build their churches, work on rancherias."

She pulled up her knees and rested her head on her crossed arms, remaining silent for a few moments before she continued. "Something happened to me, Coyote. I came here—I don't know how many days ago—and . . . the earth began to move." She lifted her arms and whipped them in the air, then jerked her torso and pointed at the ground and the rocks.

He stared at her, finally comprehending her dramatic performance. "Ah," he said, " *'emat winnp*." If she had been caught in an earthquake, that explained her injuries.

119

"After the earth stopped moving, I first came here to *this* place, but then I went back—back where we were earlier."

"Home?"

"Well, sort of. My real home is far from here, over the mountains, that way." She pointed west. "I came to the desert to visit, to stay for a few days."

He wondered if she had her own quest that had brought her here.

"So, that first day," she continued, "when I went back, my tent wasn't there and my car was gone." She cleared her throat before going on. "But then I saw . . . myself, but as a little girl. This makes no sense, I know, but I saw an old man save me and carry me up the mountain. And then I remembered how it had happened to me when I was young. I remembered it all."

"*Iichaa.*"

"Yes. It was long ago. It's so strange to say this, but the old man reminds me of you." She lifted one hand and put her fingertips on his cheek. "You have the same face."

He returned her stare.

"And the old man told me—I heard his voice in my mind—that I would be safe, always." Her eyes were filled with questions, but he saw they also held some peace, perhaps from telling him.

He nodded. "This man is *panepaaw* to me. Grandfather."

Her eyes widened and she pulled her hand away, turning to face the water again. "He's the old man I see in my dreams. I know he is. I've seen him since I was small—"

He waited, certain he knew what her next words would be.

"—and you, you're the boy I've seen, aren't you?"

Her face turned toward him and he gazed into the blue depths of her eyes, swimming in them until he saw nothing else. It was clear to him she was the white bird of *his* dreams, though he didn't quite understand how or why she could see his grandfather and him within her own dreams. He would need to speak to Grandfather about this; then, perhaps, he could try to find the words to bring some relief to her. She wanted answers, he knew, and he would try to find them for her.

"Sleep, now," he said, and pointed to the cave. "Too many words."

She nodded her agreement and rose from the rock. He followed her into the cave and waited until she had laid down. He checked the embers of the fire, then dropped onto his own blanket.

Weary from concentrating on her words and their meaning, he closed his eyes and fell asleep.

NAME: _____

ADDRESS: _____

_____

_____

TELEPHONE: _____

E-MAIL: _____

_____ I want to pay by credit card.

__ Visa          __ MasterCard          __ Discover

Account Number: _____

Expiration date: _____

SIGNATURE: _____

*Send this form, along with $2.00 shipping and handling for your FREE books, to:*

Love Spell Romance Book Club
20 Academy Street
Norwalk, CT  06850-4032

*Or fax (must include credit card information!) to:* 610.995.9274.
*You can also sign up on the Web at* <u>www.dorchesterpub.com</u>.

Offer open to residents of the U.S. and
Canada only. Canadian residents, please
call 1.800.481.9191 for pricing information.

If under 18, a parent or guardian must sign. Terms, prices and conditions
subject to change. Subscription subject to acceptance. Dorchester
Publishing reserves the right to reject any order or cancel any subscription.

# Chapter Eight

The days began to blur, melting into one another so much so that Suzanne was having difficulty keeping track of how long she'd been at the oasis. She took a piece of charcoal from the fire, one day, and decided to figure it out.

She drew a square on one of the walls of the cave and wrote the date she'd arrived at the park, then thought about each specific day she could remember something from and made a mark in the square. Figuring she had been pretty much out of it for a week when Coyote was taking care of her injuries, she concluded she'd probably been there almost a month. A month with no one even looking for her.

Logic told her there would have been search parties and helicopters flying overhead long ago. Robin had known she was here, and would have wondered why she hadn't called her on that Monday she should've been back from the week-end camping trip. Even if she'd been patient for a few days, her friend would have stopped by to check on her. She was sure of that.

What she still wasn't sure of was how to describe with any certainty exactly what had happened to her. Finally she accepted the only explanation that kept cropping up: Somehow she was no longer in her own time. And even though it was a crazy thought, nothing else fit.

Actually, most of the time she worked quite diligently to *not* think about it too much and, primarily she concentrated on raising the communication bar between her and Coyote.

Every day Coyote seemed to remember more and more English, and he became insatiable about pressing her to teach him words and phrases. They had fallen into a routine of a sort of morning lesson. She quizzed him to help him remember words, and also tried to learn some *Kumeyaay* language. He laughed at her pronunciation at times, but seemed pleased at her efforts.

"How do you say *father* in your language?" she asked as they finished cleaning the breakfast dishes and banked the fire.

"*Paataat*."

She nodded, then repeated the word. "Why is it that you never speak of him and only speak of your grandfather?"

He shot her a dark look, but remained silent.

"Bad subject?"

He pointed to the rock by the water that had become their classroom, and she followed him.

He sat, then faced the water, and she steeled herself for what she anticipated would be a serious discussion.

After a few moments, she broke the silence. "Did you learn English from your father?" She had guessed this, though only from a hunch. It seemed the only logical source.

"My father was with the white man more than with his own people," he began.

"Did he work for them?"

Coyote nodded. "On rancherias, sometimes at the missions with the padres, and he helped to bring the water out of the mountain to the people in the valley. He worked hard."

"So, why don't you ever speak of him?" She sensed discontentment in him, or worse.

"He was not good for our people. Or for me."

"What happened?" He glared at her question, then she watched his eyes soften just a little as he checked his anger.

"Why do you want to know about my father?"

She considered his question before she answered, wondering if he would understand. "I think you can know a person better if you know about their family. You've spoken to me of your grandfather, but not of your mother and father. I'm curious, I suppose."

He paused a long while and then began, his voice controlled and with a dark, sad tone. "My father brought disease to my people, what you call the smallpox. It killed my mother when I was a baby, and many of my people."

She placed her hand on his, but he pulled it away.

"He began to stay more and more with them. He would bring my people food, cloth, and supplies he'd earned. He said he wanted to make money to buy our land back from the whites who took it. They never paid him with gold, but he believed they would."

"And he taught you English when he would come home?"

"Yes. I was . . . curious. He said it would protect me if I knew the white man's language. I learned. Then, when I became a man, he asked me to go with him to see the life on the rancheria, how good it was. I stayed and worked and learned many more English words."

"Did you like it?"

"I work hard. Where I worked, a woman there had an old husband, and she wanted me to . . ."

She stared at him as his voice trailed off and he searched for words, fearing where his story was about to go.

"She asked me to come to her bed," he finally said. "It was good. She was happy. Her husband was old, and I had just become a man. He was of no use for her and wouldn't come to her bed. Later, she said I had forced her. I escaped or they would have killed me. I knew others who had been killed by the white chiefs."

"She lied about—"

"There were many lies." He shook his head

126

and glanced at her, hatred shining in his expression.

"Where was your father during this?"

"He was silent. When I saw him many moons later, he said he knew I would get away—that he was silent because *he* didn't want to be sent away. He was happy there."

"But he would still come home sometimes?"

"When for too many suns he was too drunk to work, sometimes they would send him away. He'd find us and stay for a while, and pretend to be my father. I pretended he was dead. I hated him."

"Is he still alive?"

"I heard he died of one of the white man's diseases many years ago."

"So your grandfather raised you."

"And tried to make me forgive my father, but in that he failed."

He was deeply hurt; she could see that in the tightness of his jaw and in the strain of his voice.

They remained on the rock for a long while, before he finally rose and said he was going to get firewood. They had plenty of wood; she knew he simply needed to be alone.

He had lived an existence she had only read about. Hard times were the only times for the indigenous people once the Europeans arrived. And here she was, experiencing a time through someone who knew of the struggle and atrocities firsthand.

127

Based on everything he had told her, if she was in the era she thought she was, her best guess was it was sometime in the late 1860s. A flume would have been built to bring water to Mission Valley some fifty years prior, changing the future of the area. California would have been a state for at least fifteen years, maybe more. Americans would have had their pick of land for towns, crops, and their churches.

Coyote's people would have been pushed off their own lands; those who didn't want to live with the restrictions the whites imposed would be living a nomadic life still, following their food sources along with the seasons.

She was glad he had gone for wood. The thought that she had really traveled into the past was overwhelming. Things hadn't been destroyed—everything she had been looking for hadn't vanished into thin air. It didn't even exist. At last, she had some kind of explanation, fantastic as it seemed.

*She was no longer in her own time.*

Suzanne began to put her conscious efforts toward learning all she could from Coyote about their daily existence. If she would be staying, even for a while, she needed to feel more self-sufficient.

She paid attention to his food preparation, took on the tasks of cleaning up after their meals, kept the cave swept out, even helped with the fire. He'd shown her how to keep it from burning out overnight, and lately, when he'd go off to get firewood, she ventured into the surrounding area to gather kindling. It seemed to please him, and she tried to think of things to do to keep herself from thinking too much. Her focus each day was to keep as busy as possible.

They still had their morning discussions, but she tried to keep them light, informational. And she never brought up the subject of his father again. Occasionally he'd ask questions about her home—and her people, as he would put it.

She'd tried to explain that she was a teacher, she lived alone, and that somehow in the earthquake she'd traveled to his world, his time. He seemed to easily accept what had happened with few comments, few questions.

Today the heat had been almost unbearable. It was much too hot for busy-making tasks and they'd both taken refuge in the cave to sleep through the worst heat of the day. When she'd finally awakened from her nap, she was alone. The light was dim, and Suzanne guessed it was almost evening. The temperature had dropped a little, but it was still quite warm.

When she stepped out of the cave, she saw him kneeling by the pond holding a bowl of sudsy water.

"I want to . . ."

She watched as he pointed to the bowl, then back at her. He put the bowl on the ground close to the shoreline, then pantomimed shampooing his own hair, finally patting his chest and pointing at her.

"Shampoo my hair?"

He nodded, then pointed at the suds. "What is the word?"

"Soap," she said. "Hey, is that from my yucca root?"

He nodded, pointing at his knife on the ground next to a small chunk of root. He must have brought it back to the cave the day he'd found her suffering from heat stroke and half-dead under the boulder. She'd been content to simply rinse her hair each day, sometimes scrubbing it with a little sand. Soap suds would be a treat.

She smiled and joined him by the water. He helped her lie down on a blanket he'd spread on the ground, and positioned her so that the curve of her neck was resting on a branch around which he'd wrapped several thicknesses of deerskin as padding.

Closing her eyes, she relaxed, engrossed in the feel of his fingers tugging her braid until the ends of her hair floated down and into the water. Next he wet the rest of her hair, pouring water along her scalp and working his way up to her forehead, gently shielding her eyes with one hand.

Soon she felt him pour some of the soap suds into her hair. He worked it in, massaging her scalp and squeezing the mixture throughout.

With great care, he continued to stroke and caress her long locks.

It felt wonderful. Too wonderful. She squirmed a little, resisting the urge to moan like she was on a set for the popular Organic Experience shampoo. She'd always found the commercial irritating, but she couldn't stop thinking about it, agreeing that the feel of his fingers in her hair and on her head was indeed totally sensual and intimate.

"Wrong?" he asked.

"No, perfect. Continue . . . please."

His fingers worked magic along her temples, then moved up to the top of her head, then circling down to the nape of her neck—and then he began all over again. Such strong, capable hands. *Safe.* That's what she felt most of all. Perfectly, completely safe. With him. No matter that she wasn't sure why they were together. Nothing mattered at that moment but the touch of his hands.

She was living her dream, and she knew it clearly in that instant. And she made the conscious decision right then and there to be aware of it, and to enjoy it. How rare was it that anyone ever got the chance to step into her dreamworld? And how more perfect could the situation be than one that came complete with a handsome, competent caregiver? Someone to watch over her until things changed; and sadly, the immutably logical part of her believed they would.

She sighed, and felt her face pull into a frown.

It felt as though he was almost finished—water was being poured over and over onto her head until he slowed, then squeezed the long strands. Finally, he helped her sit up.

Her scalp tingled, along with most of the rest of her. It had been pure bliss—and so she decided to return the favor.

She glanced at the bowl and saw plenty of soap suds left. "*Your* turn." She scooted herself to the edge of the blanket and nudged his shoulder, pointing at the ground.

His eyes questioned for a moment, and then he obeyed and placed the back of his neck on the branch. His black hair fell into the water as he tipped his head back as far as he could.

She picked up the small bowl he'd been using to pour with, and dipped it into the water. She wet the bulk of his hair, then placed her hand on his forehead as she worked her way to the top of his head until his hair was completely saturated.

His gaze never left her while she worked, and she felt her cheeks heat under his scrutiny. As she leaned over him, his seriousness softened and he smiled, then finally closed his eyes.

She slowly worked the suds through his hair, starting at the ends, then massaging his scalp from his forehead to the nape and back again. His face didn't reveal much, though she took the opportunity to examine it carefully. He was so still, so at ease—not a worry line anywhere.

Straight nose, prominent cheekbones—a classic, handsome, almost regal face.

His eyes flickered open, and she realized she'd stopped moving her fingers. She had no idea how long she'd been sitting there with her hands lost in his hair, staring at him.

His mouth spread into a wide smile. "Good."

She returned the smile, feeling the genuineness of his compliment, then rinsed the suds from his hair. As she squeezed out the excess water, again their eyes locked.

This time, he didn't close his eyes, and she didn't look away. She couldn't. It was as though she was being pulled deeper and deeper into his gaze. A lovely way to drown, in those eyes, she thought. Then, without thinking, she moved her hands from the back of his head to rest on his cheeks.

Still he looked at her, one eyebrow raising a fraction. "*So-SAHN?*" he whispered.

"I like it better when you call me White Bird." As she said the words, she leaned forward a little, then traced the fullness of his lower lip with her finger. His eyes drew her in even more, and before she could convince herself to stop, she brushed her lips against his. They were soft, salty. Sweet.

When she pulled back to look at him, his face had relaxed again. But his eyes looked different. They had a faraway gleam in them for an instant, then they studied her with a curious intensity.

She felt his broad hand in the middle of her back, not pulling her toward him, exactly, but making her feel she could move closer. That she should.

Leaning toward him, at last she was close enough for their lips to meet again. They melted together in a long, soft kiss. When she finally pulled away, she realized that sometime during the kiss he had moved his hands. One was nestled at the back of her head, the other grasped one of her shoulders. She felt the slightest resistance to her pulling away, then a complete relaxation of both his arms. It felt as though he had purposely given her complete control, that it was to be her decision to seek more or not.

Her lips still burned with the fire of the kiss, and she leaned forward again, this time relaxing so her chest rested on his. His hands found their way underneath her damp hair to knead her bare skin just above the deerskin wrap, and an uncontrollable moan of pleasure sounded in her throat.

She felt transported as she lowered her mouth to his, his lips massaging her own with a gentle intent, yet always waiting for her lead. She knew she was close to the point of no return. It felt so right, so wonderful; desire raced in currents through her and she began to move against him.

One of his hands dropped to her hip, and he pulled her to him. She followed the movement through so she was on top of him, then moving her hips against him, lost in the heat of his kiss and warmth of his breath on her face.

She heard a deep sound coming from him, almost a growl, and he deepened the kiss, pulling her hips against him, against his aroused body.

Breathless, she broke the embrace, pushing against his shoulders to lift the upper half of her body. His froze in response, his hands lifting from her.

"I want to take this off." She tugged at the deerskin wrapped so tightly around her, reluctant to completely break contact. Their legs had entwined and his skin was smooth and hot against hers.

He nodded and helped her sit up, to straddle him so she could get out of the wrap. When she'd tossed the deerskin aside, she saw he still kept his eyes only on hers, even though she now sat completely naked and vulnerable on top of him. Still he waited for her direction, and any remnant of restraint she might have felt, dissolved.

She reached for one of his hands and brought the fingertips to her lips, tasting them; then kissed the palm of his hand before she brought it to cup her breast, gasping at the surge of passion she felt at the touch of his hand on her.

She kept her hand on his for a moment, pressing it against her. His other hand reached up to cup her other breast, softly kneading both until she moaned with pleasure. His touch was light and almost painfully teasing. Finally, he dropped his gaze, and she watched him as he slid his hands to her waist so he could look at her fully.

She licked her lips, parched from the heat that engulfed and was between them, then reached down to tug at his loincloth. He loosened its tie with one hand, pulling it free as she shifted her hips. When she came back down against him, she felt him hard beneath her, and without hesitation, she lifted her hips again so she could lower herself onto him.

He sank deeply into her and she moaned softly, then began to move, pushing herself against him, lost in the ecstasy of their bodies moving together in perfect rhythm.

With a sense of urgency, he reached up and pulled her close, so that their bare chests rubbed together as he moved more deeply inside of her. She felt his hand on her behind, guiding her movements, positioning her so her own passion began rising within her, quickly spiraling out of control until she trembled with swell after swell, wave after wave. Then he joined her in hurtling into the icy fire, releasing a flood of raw sensation that both terrified and delighted her.

Fully spent, their bodies relaxed into one another. They were both slick with sweat; their skin melded and she couldn't feel any separateness between them.

Her cheek against his chest, she listened to the thud of his heart until it finally slowed to a normal pace. It was the lovemaking of dreams, she thought—perfect, and an act that both stripped them of energy while filling them with a kind of power.

And now that they'd finished, she felt shy again, and wondered what he thought.

"Coyote?"

"Yes, White Bird."

"Good?"

"Yes, White Bird. *'Ehan.*"

" *'Ehan.*" She whispered the word into his neck, kissing him gently. He stirred a little beneath her and she readjusted herself so that she was lying next to him with their legs still wrapped around each other, her forehead against his jaw. "Can I ask you something?" He groaned a response, and she wondered if he was asleep.

"Ask," he finally said.

"Was the white woman at the rancheria . . ."

"My only woman?" He finished her sentence for her. "No, I had a wife for a while."

"For a while?"

"I gave her no children, so she returned to her family and our marriage was over."

"How long were you together?"

"Many moons, but not so many that my heart was hurt. We were not right together. She has a new husband now, and a child. I am happy for her."

"And you didn't want another wife?"

"I go my own way. I don't stay with my people for very long—it would be wrong to take a wife."

"And you aren't lonely for your people?"

"My grandfather finds me when he wants to talk to me. I find him when I want to talk to him."

"How does he find you?" She felt him smile against her forehead.

"He calls me, here." Then she felt his finger tap on the side of her head.

He began to stroke her hair, and she closed her eyes and snuggled closer against him, longing for the moment to never end. Such a perfect moment.

# Chapter Nine

They slept in each other's embrace well into the night. When Coyote opened his eyes, White Bird's arms were still wrapped around his neck, her cheek on his chest. She felt like a feather against him, soft and weightless. As though she were a part of him.

A dream had wakened him, the pictures still vivid in his mind. He gazed at the heavens, an expanse of midnight sky that sparkled with starlight and the glow of a half moon.

*"Hellyaach sekap tewaa,"* he whispered, calling to the moon. His dream had been disturbing and left him filled with questions.

White Bird stirred, and he felt her head lift from his chest. When his gaze dropped, her eyes crinkled and smiled at him, blue eyes half-filled with sleep and her own dreams.

*"Háawka,* White Bird—hello."

*"Háawka."* Her smile deepened, and she

looked up to the night sky then back at him. "It must be late. We slept."

"Swim now?" he asked.

"Lovely idea." She pushed against him and was up and into the water by the time he rose to join her.

The pool was silky against his skin, and he swam the length of the pond a few times, still trying to clear his head of the dream. Finally he joined her in the middle of the water where she was standing, only her head and shoulders visible. He dropped his feet to the bottom to stand facing her, and the water lapped at their shoulders.

"Coyote, I feel like we should talk about . . ." Her voice trailed off, and she looked down at the water.

Reaching for her chin, he lifted it so he could see her eyes. "Sorry?"

"No, no—I'm confused, I guess. I don't know how to feel, or how you feel about what happened between us."

"*Shuullaw.*" He closed his eyes to search for the word in her language. When he found it, he opened his eyes and tipped his head to one side. "Thunder. Like good thunder."

Her eyes widened in response, and her face relaxed. He was pleased to have found the right word to express how he felt. It had been more than good to be with her. Better, in fact, than he could ever remember experiencing. Better than he could imagine it ever could be with any woman. He leaned closer, so he could kiss the smile on her lips.

When their lips touched, he wanted her all over again, but he resisted the impulse to pull her close to him, to reach for the thunder again. He needed to tell her about the dream.

When their lips parted, he began. "A dream woke me."

"Just now? You want to tell me about it?"

"*Haa*. Yes."

She moved back a step to create some space between them, and nodded. "Okay."

"Messages came to me. Messages about my journey and why I am here in this place. I must go away for . . ." He paused, holding up one hand, his fingers extended.

"Five?" she prompted.

"Five suns."

"Okay. Is there a problem?"

"You would be alone."

"I would be fine alone."

He looked away for a moment. That's what had disturbed him so much. Even though it was critical he resume his quest, his dream also spoke of the danger in leaving her behind—but it was unclear what kind of danger. There was no good solution.

"I know how to keep the fire. You've taught me well. You can gather enough wood for five days. And you can show me how to make *shawii*. I don't need much food in this heat, anyway."

He considered her words carefully. She indeed

had grown much more capable in the last several days; she was right. He had no real argument other than what he felt inside, what his heart told him.

"So, you should go," she said.

Her words had a definite tone of finality and he knew the discussion had concluded. Over the next few days he would prepare for the journey, show her how to make the food she would need while he was gone, and try to convince her not to stray too far from the cave.

After they'd finished stacking the last of the firewood, Suzanne watched Coyote gather the supplies he would be taking on his journey. She missed him already, part of her wishing she had tried at least a little to talk him out of leaving, or suggest he put it off for a while.

They'd grown closer since they'd made love, talking more, spending more time learning about each other. Now at night he slept next to her, and she often woke in the morning with his arm draped over her. He hadn't reached for her during the coolness of the nights, but every morning he'd smile shyly and whisper *shuullaw* in her ear, bringing goosebumps to her skin and a long shudder of pleasure as her body remembered their lovemaking.

She could ask him to stay, and he probably would. But though she was tempted, she resisted the urge. He had come to the oasis as part of his own journey, only to be delayed by the task of nursing her back to health. He had something to finish, obviously something of great meaning to him. And she had a feeling it was something far bigger than she could ever comprehend.

So, rather than let him see the regret in her face, she avoided looking at him while he gathered his supplies. Instead, she busied herself making their dinner. She decided to make *shawii* with bits of meat and some dried seeds as his send-off meal, something hearty. He would be traveling during the cool of the night, and planned to leave as soon as the moon rose.

She felt him watching her as she scooped some of the acorn meal from a storage basket, then put it into a cooking pot. She added water until it was the consistency of oatmeal, then dropped in bits of dried meat and seeds and a generous pinch of salt. She sat by the low fire, stirring the mixture as it heated and thickened.

By the time the dinner was ready, he was too. He wasn't taking much—a small net that he filled with water gourds, his rabbit stick, and a few other containers that probably held some dried food, she guessed. Before he closed up the net, he added a few of his medicine bags.

She handed him a bowl of food, then served herself and joined him where he now sat, on the rock by the pond. They ate silently, staring at the still water and watching the shadows lengthen in the late afternoon sunshine.

"Good," he said. "Good *shawii*."

"You're a good teacher."

"I think you must also be good teacher. Tell me about your school."

Her students were her first thoughts. She was surprised she missed them so much. Summer sessions would just be starting, and she would normally be gearing up to teach an intensive course in the ecology of native plants of San Diego County. It was one of her favorites, with many classes held in the field and out of the stuffy classrooms. "I love to teach. My students learn about plants, how to keep them safe."

He nodded his approval. "*Millychish* don't know plants and trees like *Kumeyaay*. White men build on good land and many plants die."

It was true. Many native plants were hard to find. Some had disappeared completely, and some were still around but in inaccessible places. The prognosis was often bleak. "I went to the Barona reservation once, and through an interpreter—"

He stopped her and said, "I don't know this word."

"Someone who knows both English and *Kumeyaay*. I asked the elders about plants they had gathered when they were young. Their eyes grew sad, and they told me about plants they could no longer find, plants that they feared were gone forever."

"*Millychish*." His voice a whisper, but harsh in its tone.

"My students will help protect the land and the plants. They are good *millychish*."

144

"Like you," he said. "There is always a person like you in our village, one who knows each plant, when to put the seeds in the ground, and all the things to know about it."

She looked at him, but he didn't meet her gaze. Though his tone sounded casual, she heard the earnestness with which he said the words. It was not light praise. "I do care what happens to the plants here, and the plants where my home is. My teaching is a good thing, an important thing."

"The plant healer in my village is old now. Maybe you will meet her someday . . . if you do not go home." He put down his bowl and turned to face her. "While I am gone, stay close to the water."

His eyes revealed his deep concern for her, and she put her hand on his cheek. "I'll be fine. Don't worry about me."

He nodded, then put his arm around her waist and pulled her closer. They sat side by side in comfortable silence as the darkness crept over them, until at last it was time for him to leave.

# Chapter Ten

Suzanne spent the night catnapping. Every time she dozed off, she'd jolt awake and reach for the empty spot on Coyote's blanket.

"Well, this is ridiculous." If it continued, she'd be completely sleep deprived by the time he got back. She finally gave up as the first rays of morning light filtered into the cave.

The day ahead of her already seemed too long to comprehend, with too many empty hours to fill. She wasn't used to feeling such longing for someone.

She had always loved being alone, for the most part. She'd always cherished her solo camping trips, her escapes from the daily routine to snatch an hour off by herself on a park trail or simply on a walk in her neighborhood.

Now she found she couldn't stop thinking about him. Him and the feel of his body next to hers, she admitted. The intensity of the bond that

147

had formed between them was almost unnerving. *And impossible*, she thought.

She looked more closely at how she was really feeling. Was the intensity simply infatuation? A side-effect of her own confusion? Perhaps. And worse than the infatuation was the fact that she was beginning to feel emotionally dependent on him, which conflicted with the essence of who she was. And if she were being honest with herself, she was also fooling herself if she thought there was really a future for them. It just wasn't logical. A future for her and a *Kumeyaay* warrior?

It was much more likely that she would somehow return to her own time, and he would return to his people. A relationship wasn't fair to him either, and she decided to set aside the time to explain that to him when he returned.

Her head felt clearer than it had in days, and she reasoned that the time apart would no doubt be good for them both.

By noon, the cave floor was devoid of even a stray blade of grass, the fire was banked for the rest of the day, she'd finished her lunch, and she was sick of obsessing about the entire situation.

And then the cramps came.

The positive was, at least she wasn't pregnant. She had successfully ignored the quiet fears that surfaced about the fact that they'd had sex sans contraception. A part of her had embraced the fantasy that it would be impossible for her to conceive within her dreamworld, in this time before time.

Actually, the reality of her period's appearance made her immediately and immensely thankful. And the feeling of gratitude was quickly followed by the realization that she had been a real idiot. Where was her brain? Had she lost all common sense?

She checked for stains on her inner thigh—now what was she supposed to do? Indian women left their village during menstruation, she knew, but she was ignorant of any of the details of exactly what they did during that time. It simply wasn't something she'd ever heard discussed or read about.

She rummaged through the containers and bags Coyote had left behind in the cave, looking for something she might use for a pad. In a large leather sack she found several pieces of a muslin type of cloth, and then a long piece of leather string.

With those she fashioned a sort of breechcloth—folding one of the long pieces of cloth she'd found and placing it between her legs, finally tying the leather string around her waist to secure both ends of the cloth. Unwrapping her deerskin, she checked for stains, thankful she wasn't yet flowing very heavily. Her homemade pad and belt worked perfectly.

The cramps worsened just as she secured the pad, and she wondered if Coyote had also left any medicinal herbs behind. Once again, she searched through the supplies until she found several small bundles. Opening each carefully, she smelled them all until she found the one she was hoping she'd find. *Sage.*

She added some kindling and branches to the fire, then poked it enough to ignite the wood so she could heat a container of water and make some tea. She placed a flat stone near the embers to warm, then fashioned a heating pad by wrapping the stone in a piece of sheepskin she found.

*All the comforts of home.* Her cramps slowly subsided as the heat of the stone relaxed her muscles.

Now she was eternally grateful Coyote was gone, glad she had managed on her own. Glad to be dealing with reality again. The last few days had been far too dreamy, and not enough based in fact. *Too perfect.* Like any other fantasy, she needed to realize it probably wouldn't last.

Moving her rabbitskin blanket next to the pond, she spent the rest of the afternoon there and sipped the sage tea as needed to deal with the pain of her cramps. She stayed quiet, and observed the birds and animals that visited the pond to drink. As evening came, she stayed by the pool, and settled in a comfortable spot sitting by a palm tree with her back against its trunk, her legs outstretched so her toes could dip into the cool water.

Her eyes adjusted to the dimming light and she decided to remain where she was, to see what creatures would come. Usually she and Coyote were inside the cave preparing dinner about that same time, and she was curious what animals she'd have the chance to observe.

Her attention was drawn to movement on the far side of the pond, and she squinted to see what was there. Several squirrels appeared. Their round tails were long and slender, not bushy like the city squirrels she fed peanuts to in Balboa Park on Sundays, and they actually looked more like stripeless chipmunks. These were round-tailed ground squirrels, hearty enough to survive the desert heat, able to live on the seeds and insects for which they scavenged. They were cinnamon-colored, so unlike their gray city cousins. Several skittered close to the water to drink, then quickly scampered back into the brush.

Less than three yards to her left, a desert cottontail approached but kept a careful eye on Suzanne. He looked healthy, about a foot long with moderately long ears that weren't nearly as furry as a domestic rabbit's. His fur was buff brown, but he had a white chest and tail, and the back of his neck was a lovely rust color.

Just like her fur blanket.

"Sorry, Mr. Bunny," she whispered. His ears flicked at the sound of her voice, but he remained. Satisfied he wasn't in any imminent danger, he drank from the shallow water, then hopped away. *Coyote probably would have thrown his rabbit stick at you for our dinner, Mr. Bunny.*

*Better not stop by when there are hungry humans about.*

Several birds flew by and into the shadows while she watched, but it was too dark to make out their species. One looked like a woodpecker, but the sound of a piercing *keee-ar* followed by *flicka-flicka-flicka* hinted it was a northern flicker instead.

Her vigil continued as the crescent moon made its appearance, and with it, she spotted the silhouette of a great horned owl as it flew over the water. A rodent of some sort dangled limply from its beak. The owl landed on a nearby branch that hung out over the water, and rapidly swallowed its dinner. Then its great head turned toward her, the outline of its ear tufts clear in the moonlight, its golden eyes shining.

At the sound of its deep *hoo-hoo-hoo*, her eyes felt suddenly heavy, and Suzanne found she could no longer keep her eyelids from drooping. In an instant, her body felt three times its normal weight, and she didn't think she had the strength to stand. Succumbing to the hypnotic and potent pull of sleep, she curled up on the ground, her intention only to close her eyes for a few minutes until she felt able to make her way to the cave.

*She walked as slowly as she could toward the main building, the pine trees on either side towering at least a hundred feet high, maybe higher. They were wonderful old trees.*

*It was a log building, but not a primitive one. More*

like the expensive log homes showcased in the chic architecture magazines she'd thumbed through recently at her dentist's office—designed to look rustic, but actually quite modern in construction. Comfortable and, most likely, energy efficient.

It was a good design for the location, and the building looked like it belonged; more like a part of the environment, rather than a man-made structure plunked down in the middle of a forest. Great care had been taken with this concept, and it showed.

A man with long gray hair stood in the open door.

"Welcome, Suzanne, I've been waiting for you. Would you like to take a look around?"

She nodded. Such a kind face; he looked as though he belonged in this forest, too, and she liked him immediately.

They didn't speak, but it was as though they were conversing while they walked side-by-side through many buildings. Some of the structures held classrooms, one housed a formidable library, and an adjacent room was filled with the latest computers. There were impressive, well-equipped laboratories and comfortable study environments sprinkled throughout; cozy nooks with wingback chairs and laptops on sidetables awaiting a student looking for an intimate setting in which to study.

The last building housed several classrooms that led into an attached greenhouse filled with starter flats, seedlings, and countless varieties of plants in various stages of growth.

Garden carts and tools lined one wall, and a pile of fragrant black soil awaited empty pots.

"What do you think?" the man asked.

"It's perfect—a beautiful campus and the accommodations seem top notch and state-of-the-art," she replied.

He nodded, agreeing with her assessment. "You'll need to tell them soon, you know."

"I know. I will."

"Do you want to stay here a while?"

"That would be nice." He left, then, and she wandered farther into the greenhouse and saw a door. When she pushed it open, she found herself walking into another even larger structure—an indoor garden. It was an ecosystem, she realized, complete with mature plants, trees, and even birds.

On a nearby aspen branch, a butterfly landed. As its lemon-yellow wings fluttered open and it stilled, the black stripes distinguished it as a western tiger swallowtail.

"Well, aren't you beautiful," she whispered, watching it for a few seconds before it folded its wings and fluttered away toward the high, glass ceiling.

She stepped onto a flagstone path and followed its winding course to a pond at the far end of the structure. There she sat on a bench to watch the fish swim. Then her thoughts were interrupted by the high-pitched musical trill of a toad. She peered along the water's edge until she saw a flattish body covered with small reddish bumps. It was unmistakably a male red-spotted toad.

"What are you doing here, so far from home?"

She might ask herself the same question, she thought.

154

So far from home. *Could* she *be as content in this place? Everything was here that the little toad needed: constant water, a balanced environment, some sort of food source, and not a enemy in sight. He should be quite happy within his glass paradise among the trees.*

*And so should she.*

*The toad took a mighty leap into the pond, and disappeared.*

The sound of water roused her, and Suzanne opened her eyes a crack, careful not to move. A few feet away, a large gray dog was drinking at the edge of the pond. *Not* a dog. *A coyote.* Surely he must have smelled her, she thought, but obviously he considered her non-threatening enough to stay for a much-needed drink.

The animal lapped at the water's edge for several moments before he stopped and glanced her way. He seemed to accept her presence completely. Then he dropped to his belly as though exhausted from a long journey. Coyotes were known to travel for hundreds of miles, and she wondered where this one had been, where he might have come from.

Back home, daily newscasts warned coyotes were getting more and more aggressive as their habitats shrunk, and it wasn't unusual for local anchors to show tape of one roaming a suburban neighborhood. A friend had lost his best pal, Gus, a loveable Yorkie, in his own back yard to a bold coyote that had hopped the fence with ease and ended the dog's life in one murderous bite.

She shuddered at the memory, and kept her eyes almost closed to avoid giving the animal the impression she might be confronting him. Remaining as still as possible, she watched the creature's eyes grow heavy, and he finally dropped his head onto his paws to rest, wrapping his bushy black-tipped tail around his body much like any domestic canine.

He slept for at least half an hour, she guessed, before he stirred. First she noticed one of his ears twitch; a second later his head lifted up and he was instantly alert. Off in the distance, she heard a series of barks and yelps, and then a prolonged howl.

Was it a howl he recognized?

The coyote lifted his grizzled chest up so he sat on his haunches, then tipped his head back, his nose in the air. He yipped and howled in response to the distant call. And the sound was beautiful. Not frightening. Musical, in its own wildness.

Suzanne opened her eyes fully, knowing he would leave soon to perhaps rendezvous with another. He turned, as if to go, but stopped in mid-stride. She watched as his tail wagged and his head turned to look at her over his shoulder—as though to say farewell, or in thanks for sharing the waterhole.

He ambled off down the trail and out of sight. A few seconds later, his howl echoed in the canyon and brought goosebumps to her skin. Her eardrums quivered with the sound, his voice implanted in her memory forever.

Sitting up, she stretched her arms and legs, stiff from being in the same position too long, then returned to the cave for the remainder of the night. As she spread out her blanket, she felt the tug of homesickness. Bits and pieces of the dream about the university lingered, and as the pictures became clearer, she thought about the pending job offer for the first time since she'd been at the oasis, for the first time since she'd opened herself up to Coyote.

They probably thought she'd fallen off the face of the earth. Or worse. She envisioned her answering machine filled with messages from the chancellor, wondering why she hadn't let them know her final decision about the job.

She lay for a long time, sleep eluding her, and she began to daydream about what she would do if she *could* go home—particularly if Coyote could come with her.

First, she'd have to decline the university's offer, because he would be more comfortable in the San Diego area—though he'd probably find her one-bedroom apartment too confining. But they wouldn't need to stay there, she thought. They could move away from the city, east toward the mountains where they could find a place with some land and not too many neighbors. Something that bordered some open space, perhaps, so he would feel more at home.

It would be a difficult transition for someone like him. No, she admitted, it might be impossible for someone like him, but she thought he might try.

Her thoughts germinated into a new one, just as the pull of sleep finally came: Tomorrow she would venture from the oasis to explore a little more, to search for signs of any other paths they might have missed. To see if there was any way to somehow get back to what she knew. More than ever, she needed to know if she was ever going back.

# Chapter Eleven

By the fourth day of Coyote's absence, Suzanne had methodically explored in every direction with no new results—there was no sign of civilization within a half a day's walking distance of the oasis.

Each day she'd gotten up as soon as there was enough light to see the ground, and returned before the heat of the noonday sun was at its worst. On each trail she'd created a series of markers, stones piled in specific patterns to mark the areas she'd already explored, careful to periodically look over her shoulder as she walked so she was always aware of the landmarks to look for on her way back.

Mindful of the serious threat of dehydration, each day she carried a water gourd and even a little bit of food. She'd even studied the weave of her sandals so she could fashion a head-covering made of woven strips of dry yucca leaves. She tied it on her head using the leather string she no longer needed around her waist to secure her sanitary pad. Though she was certain it looked foolish, she knew it was the smart thing to do to keep her head shaded from the harsh desert sun.

On the fifth day, she decided to venture down the main path, sure that Coyote would have taken it on his quest and would return by it. She'd take a full water gourd and meet him. It would be a sweet homecoming, and she was eager to hear of his adventure.

She found a secure spot that even offered a bit of shade, and waited the entire day for him.

When the sun dipped below the peaks, she reluctantly headed back toward the oasis to make dinner, something she could keep warm on the fire for him if he arrived later in the evening. A feeling of apprehension nagged at her, and she wondered if he had run into any trouble along the way. Why was he late in returning?

He could take care of himself, and it was silly to think otherwise, she told herself. She shook away any lingering thoughts of impending disaster that might be awaiting him, and headed for the palm trees in the distance, thinking about what she could do differently with acorn flour and the seeds and meat bits left in the food supplies.

As she neared the last bend in the path, she thought she could hear voices. Though it seemed unlikely, she stopped to listen anyway, crouching on the path to peer around a boulder.

Definitely men's voices.

Removing her headgear, she cupped her hand around one ear, tipped her head, then slowly leaned out from behind the rock in order to hear more clearly what they were saying.

Two men stood in front of the cave entrance, and she watched as they both squatted so they could peer inside. They wore wide-brimmed hats pulled down low on their heads so it was difficult to see their faces, but one appeared to be clean-shaven, and the other had a thick, long beard. Both wore long-sleeved shirts buttoned to the neck, and pants with holes in the knees tucked into high boots turned down at the tops.

And each wore a belt with a revolver tucked into it.

"You're absolutely certain this is the right cave."

"Aw, Pete, all I know is that he said the Indian would meet us in the cave by the palms with a sample of the gold. I don't know no other palm trees in this godforsaken hellhole."

"Then it should be the right one. But it looks to me as though more than one person is actually living here."

The clean-shaven man entered the cave, then called out to the other. "Mac, come in here."

The bearded one disappeared into the cave, so Suzanne crept silently to a boulder that offered a perfect vantage point for listening but where she would still be hidden from view.

"There are two blankets, definitely two people. And definitely Indian gear."

"Maybe he's huntin'."

"His bow and arrows are here, so I have my doubts."

"Well, they can't be far—"

As Suzanne moved a step closer, she heard the distinct and very close sound of a snake's rattle—and threw herself out from behind the boulder in sheer fright, tumbling onto the path in front of the cave.

By the time she got her feet under her to run, the two men had already rushed out, guns drawn.

"Well, looky here . . ." The bearded one's mouth gaped open as he lifted his gun.

She avoided looking at their weapons, and instead looked up at the faces of the men.

"Mac, I'll do the talking." Pete, the clean-shaven one, stepped closer to her. "Do you speak English?"

She nodded, her heart thudding in her ears. "What do you want?"

"Where is the Indian?" he asked.

"I don't know what you mean. I'm alone." Her mind raced, trying to understand if Coyote could possibly be the one they'd been talking about. Somehow she doubted it. Surely he would have told her about a meeting with these men.

"You think she's in on it?" Mac stepped closer

and tipped his gun up so that it was within inches of her nose.

"Mac, you be good, now. I need to think for a minute."

Mac stepped back obediently, and dropped his weapon a little. Obviously Pete was in charge, so she turned her full attention to him.

"In on what?" she asked, trying to keep her voice as neutral as possible.

"Someone was supposed to meet us here. Where's the Indian? And I'd rather not have to ask you again." His eyes darkened and he took a step closer.

"He was here, and now he's gone back to his village," she said, meeting the man's stare with as much boldness as she could muster.

He reacted by slapping her hard on the cheek, and her knees buckled from the shock. His open hand left a stinging on her face.

"Not likely he's away without his bow, miss. What are you doing with a redskin, anyway?"

"He . . ." She searched for the right thing to say, her mind blanking.

"Speak up, miss. Are you expecting him to-day?"

"I have no idea." With any luck, Coyote would hear the voices, and approach the oasis with caution.

"You know about the gold?" Mac asked.

"*Mac—*"

"Well, she *must* know about it if she's here."

In a lightning-fast movement, Pete whirled and struck the other man on the side of the head with the barrel of his gun, sending him reeling backward several steps. When Mac reached his hand up and then brought it away, Suzanne saw that it was covered with blood.

"Another word, and it'll be far worse the next time," Pete said calmly. His voice was hard.

With her hand still covering her burning cheek, Suzanne watched Mac pull a bandanna from his pocket and hold it against his head wound, his lower lip quivering a little. Then Pete returned his attention to her.

"Since my companion here has broached the subject, are you aware of why we are here?"

"If you're asking me if I know anything about any gold, then the answer is no. I don't know what you're talking about."

"She's lyin', Pete!"

"Quiet, you idiot." Pete's voice was rough, and he sighed with exasperation. "One more word from you and I swear I'll cut you out of the deal completely. Do you understand me?"

Mac hung his head. "I don't mean no harm, Pete."

Pete ignored the apologetic response. Instead, he continued to stare at her, obviously considering his next move with great care. "Get up and fix us something to eat."

She rose, kept her gaze on the ground, then walked past him and into the cave, relieved to be farther away from them both. Better that they thought her meek and subservient now; it might give her an advantage later.

They remained outside by the pond, talking in low voices, and though she tried with all her might to make out what they were saying, she couldn't understand a word.

*Coyote, where are you? I don't know what to do.*

As she angrily stoked the fire, a spark flew and landed on the back of her wrist. She bit her lip to keep from crying out and, instead, dipped a rag into some water and wrapped it around the burn. While she gathered what she needed to cook, she continued to send Coyote mental messages—both calling for help and warning him of the danger.

Within a few minutes she had prepared a plain meal of *shawii*, and when it was ready, she called out to the men. They sat next to the low fire and she handed each a bowl, then sat on her blanket as far away as she could get.

"You'd better eat something, too," Pete said, nodding at the food left in the cook pot.

"I'm not hungry."

"Eat."

"No, thank you."

Pete kicked an empty bowl toward her. "If your Indian friend doesn't arrive tonight, my companion here will be transporting you to a holding area. You will, indeed, be quite sorry if you don't eat something now."

She frowned at him but held her tongue, then picked up the bowl from the ground and stepped closer to the fire to serve herself dinner. As she leaned forward, she felt a painful tug on her braid. "*Ow!*"

She looked up and saw the gleam of a knife blade in one of Pete's hands, and in the other, at least six inches of her hair. He had cut off the end of her braid.

"This will work fine to prove to your friend that you are in our possession. I am confident he'll be much more cooperative—wouldn't you agree, Mac?"

With her knees so rubbery she was amazed she could even walk, she managed to turn away from the men and return to her blanket, determined to eat her meal and gather her strength for whatever might come next.

# Chapter Twelve

Coyote had waited for two days, sitting motionless in the shade of a granite slab where Grandfather had instructed him to go. He had remained still, sipped only water, and turned inward as he prepared himself for his vision quest.

Finally, he felt ready.

*Grandfather?*

*Yes, my grandson.*

*Is the time right?*

*What does your heart say?*

*My heart tells me to ask you.*

*And you have. When you drink the* tolvaach *on this day and take your journey, you will be transformed. You will be able to fly with the wind and you may visit many worlds that are unknown to you.*

*Will you be there to guide me?*

*No, Hattepaa, this journey you will take alone. But you will not be entirely alone.*

*What do you mean, Grandfather?*

*Spirit beings may appear to help you along the way . . . or to tempt you.*

*Will I know the difference?*

*Fly with your heart, Hattepaa, and you must watch and listen with your soul and remember all that you have learned. All should be well. Call to me if you need me.*

*Thank you, Grandfather. Will this quest tell me what I wish to know?*

*Yes, my grandson. Yes.*

As he felt Grandfather's spirit fade, Coyote reached for the small gourd that hung by a braided rope at his waist, undid the lid and peered inside. It was more jimsonweed elixir than he'd ever ingested before. And it was stronger. The mixture would bring many visions, or it would kill him.

Though he was eager for the experience to come, fear still squeezed his heart as he settled himself against the rock wall, his back straight as a tree, his legs outstretched.

The rock wall above him was covered with paintings. It was a sacred place that he and Grandfather had first visited when he was just a boy. He hadn't been at all sure he would even be able to find it for his vision quest, but it was as though his feet clearly knew the way.

When he'd arrived, he'd climbed up to take a closer look at the paintings. Some were old, others looked oddly fresh—so much so that he wondered if his grandfather had been here recently.

With one finger he'd traced the red outline of

the head of the life-sized horned figure, one he remembered well from his first visit when he was a boy. It was the figure's black eyes that had frightened him the most.

Grandfather had promised to bring him back to the sacred place that winter, on the shortest day, the solstice day. They had arrived just before sunrise, and Grandfather had told him to look at the black eyes of the great horned figure. He'd been troubled, and wondered if the figure would come to life on that special day. Grandfather had simply urged him to be patient, to wait. And as the sun rose and the first rays peeked out from behind a nearby mountain, a dagger of light shone on the black eyes.

Only on this day does this happen, Grandfather had said, and now you have seen this thing. It was then that he'd understood that Grandfather would be his teacher. From him he would learn many strange things, many wonderful things. And he had.

His fingers next touched his favorite painting: a man riding a bobcat. He had been mesmerized by it as a child and it still fascinated him. Next to that was his own faded black handprint.

He placed his hand over the print, remembering the day he'd left it. It had been after he'd become a man. Grandfather had brought him to the wall and Coyote had chosen a spot close to the little bobcat.

His black handprint was now quite faded, but

next to it was a bright red handprint, its slender fingers so close they almost touched his. Someone had to have been there very recently for the color to be so bright, and he wondered who else came to the site. He'd never seen any other people, only the addition of paintings each time Grandfather had brought him.

More new paintings were above the red handprint, also fresh. Two people: a man and a woman. The male figure was elaborate in its black, red and white paint. It had seemed familiar, and he'd wondered if he'd seen one like it before. The female figure was red, with white lines coming out of her head. Not like the horned figure, but not like any other figure he'd ever seen, or any other drawings he remembered. He would ask Grandfather about them the next time they visited the wall together.

At the top of the wall, too high to get close to, was a fantastic depiction of the sun. It was also new, its white paint gleaming. The circle was filled with a spider's web, and straight lines of uneven length protruded around the circumference. It was magnificent, well deserved of the uppermost position.

Now was the time.

Coyote brought the gourd to his lips and drank the liquid until it was gone. He closed his eyes, strangely at peace now that he had taken the elixir.

At first he felt nothing, only the cool of the stone against his back; then he realized the wall seemed less solid. Instead of the familiar cold hardness, it felt as though he were leaning against something cushioned, something padded. The softness hugged his back, and he began to relax against it.

And then he was inside the rock.

Inside, it still wasn't solid—somehow, it was like liquid rock. He stared at his own arm, then looked at his body and saw that he, too, had become liquid, though he could still make out the outline of his form.

He was both liquid and shining light. His skin glowed, and it was as though his body had become like the living embers of a dying fire. He was all colors: red and yellow and blue and white. He felt no heat, no cold, only a strange vibration that tingled as he moved.

But the dominant feeling he had was that he belonged. He understood that he was part of the rock . . . because he had *wanted* to be.

He considered the idea for a moment or for hours, he couldn't tell.

And then he thought of the sky.

He felt his body melt and pass through the surface of the rock wall, then drift up toward the fading sun until he was riding the wind.

At first he followed the flight of the birds that shared the sky, dipping and soaring as they chased each other and as they dove toward prey far below on the desert floor. He flew with the eagle and the hawk until he became a brother to them and they gladly showed him their hunting grounds and the safe places to sleep.

And then he looked up.

As he wondered where the sky ended, he felt his lightness become even lighter than the wind. He became the air that all creatures breathe.

And the higher he thought, the higher he was. The blue of the sky became blacker than any other night he'd seen. Dazzling points of light followed him in the blackness, light that danced like sunlight dances on the surface of almost-still water.

He was afraid to look down, and instead closed his eyes and thought of the ocean.

His lightness became liquid again, cool and silky and instantly he was among the animals and plants of the sea. He was all the colors of the water, his own color changing as he moved from deep to shallow to deep again. He swam with *'ehpank*, the largest of sea animals. And he became a brother to the immense gray giant. And when his brother opened his huge mouth to drink in the water filled with food, he went inside him.

There he connected with the innermost being of the creature, and understood its wisdom—and, within the briefest of moments, experienced its entire lifetime and that of its species. Then, finally, he felt its enormous love and its synergy with the Earth Mother.

When the creature's mouth opened, Coyote rushed out with the water and onto the shore of the land. His body became solid again and he walked along the beach toward a man who waited for him.

As he grew nearer, he saw that it was his father.

"My son, I have been waiting for you."

"I am here."

"And my heart sings to see you."

Coyote didn't respond; anger filled his soul and prevented him from speaking.

"I have something to say to you, my son."

Coyote waited.

"Will you sit with me?"

Coyote nodded. Then he sat opposite his father on the sand with his knees touching his father's knees, the way he'd sat as a boy when his father would tell him stories of his adventures and what he did when he was far away from their village.

"My son, in my life I have many regrets. I was blinded by things that you will not understand, but that is not what I wish to speak of today."

In an instant Coyote felt his father's sadness rush over him like a river flooding its banks in a storm.

"I cannot change what has passed, but there is an emptiness in my heart and in yours that we cannot fill without each other."

Several minutes passed, or maybe days. Time was different within the vision world.

His father waited patiently, until at last his image began to fade into nothingness. Then he was gone.

And Coyote hadn't said what was in his own heart, his own soul. It had been time wasted. He leaned his head back and closed his eyes, and he screamed a scream that finally emptied the anger from his body.

He screamed until he had no breath, then lay back on the sand to gaze at the darkened sky. He felt the heat of another body next to him.

"Grandson, why do you scream a scream that fills the sky?"

"I am confused, Grandfather. Why did my father come?"

"I will not know the answers to your questions, my grandson. Those you must ask yourself, and not me."

"My journey has been so beautiful—more wondrous than I imagined it could ever be, but I still do not know my path."

"Then perhaps your journey is not yet complete. Rest now, and wait."

His grandfather's presence faded, and Coyote stretched out his arms and legs in the sand, still gazing at the dazzling night sky.

He stared at the stars and soon floated among them, looking down upon the land and then, upon his people. As he wondered what his people were doing, he began to fall from the sky, closer and closer to the ground until he floated just above the towering pine trees of one of their mountain villages. It was the one he remembered most from his childhood.

As he looked at his people he recognized his

aunt and some cousins, boys he had played with before he'd left his village when he'd become a man. Then the leader of his people gathered everyone into a large circle. While no sounds were audible, Coyote began to *feel* their questions.

His attention was drawn to a small boy who turned away from the crowd. The boy tipped his head, then lifted his eyes up toward the trees, toward Coyote. And their eyes locked. A smile filled the boy's face until Coyote sensed it reached all the way to his small heart. And as Coyote watched him, the boy began to glow— scarlet and purple waves of color pulsated outside his body, drawing Coyote to float down, closer and closer.

Then the boy lifted his hand to extend one finger. Coyote reached out, and a wave of red and purple left the boy and traveled to his own outstretched hand in a lightning bolt of color.

The color filled him. It sizzled as it surged through his veins until he thought he wouldn't be able to tolerate it a moment more; then a wave of coolness followed which saturated him with renewed energy . . . and hope for his people.

*My people.*

The boy's colors faded as the boy turned away, his attention back on the leader.

Coyote rose, floating back to the treetops, and behind his closed eyes, he began to think of the rock wall. He thought of the wall until once again he felt himself inside it, and then he remembered his body sitting against the wall. Soon he felt the familiar heaviness of his earthbound flesh-and-blood body; loud in his ears he heard the sound of his blood racing through veins, the beating of his heart, and the new song of his soul.

Coyote woke.

His eyes opened on a black sky heavy with stars, and when he looked down to the desert floor, the moon's glow on the sand sparkled with its own light as though it were competing with the heavens.

His mind felt so numb, the task of thinking seemed insurmountable.

For hours, he simply stared at the sky and watched the darkness lighten until the stars, one by one, faded to nothingness, replaced at last with the rosy pink of morning.

He lifted his arm, bringing a hand to his lips, and his fingertips told him they were dry and cracked from days without water. When he tried to moisten them, his swollen tongue refused to move.

A crunching sound pulled his gaze, and he saw his water gourd empty and rolling in the morning breeze. He would need to find some kind of moisture—and quickly, before his ability to think completely dissolved.

As he brought his hand down, his fingertips touched wetness. Too weary to move his head, he brought his fingers back to his lips and sucked the droplets. Water. Cool, sweet water.

*Grandfather?*

There was no answer.

Again and again, he dipped his fingers into the wetness and brought them back to his lips. When he was finally able to move, he turned to see that a large shallow *olla* sat on the ground next to him, an *olla* he didn't recognize as his. And it was filled to overflowing with fresh water, water that had somehow stayed cool in the growing heat of the day.

His *first* day.

Nothing would ever be the same, of this he was certain. He picked up the vessel and brought it to his lips, its coolness soothing his parched throat and sending relief singing through his body. When he had drained it, he put the bowl down, and gingerly got to his feet.

His legs were just able to keep him erect, and he leaned against the rock wall until he felt secure enough to take the few steps he needed to in order to reach his supplies.

He sat again as soon as he reached the containers that still held the dried rabbit he'd brought with him. With his first meal in days, his strength began to return.

He would rest one more night before the journey back to the oasis.

# Chapter Thirteen

Coyote awoke with a scream in his throat, his body covered in cold sweat. He stood, gathered his supplies, and began to run. It was a few hours until dawn and, if he kept a steady pace, he would be back at the cave by daybreak.

As he ran, he played the dream over and over in his mind.

He was flying, and a white-winged bird flew with him, circling him as they both rose higher and higher in the sky. Then the wings of the bird began to glow so brightly that he could no longer look upon it, and he closed his eyes.

But he could still feel the bird, sensing every flap of its wings, every dip it made in the sky, every circle it made around him. He and the bird were as one, and he was completely saturated with the feeling of its luminescence.

And then he sensed something was terribly wrong. When he opened his eyes, the bird was in a metal cage and the cage was filled with

179

flames. When he looked below him, he saw his people were gathered and unaware of a fire that raged within the forest—a wildfire with a path leading directly toward their village. If he could warn them, there would be time to take refuge in a nearby stream.

His thought was that he would first save the bird—but when he extended his hand to unlock the cage, the fire within jumped through the air setting him, too, ablaze. He fell to the earth, unable to warn the village. It, too, was soon engulfed in flames, the sound of the villagers' horrified screams filling his ears.

It had been those images and sounds of death that had awakened him.

The meaning seemed clear: White Bird was in trouble. He would go to her but, unlike in the dream, he would get there in time to save her.

He ran through the day and night, only stopping for sips of water when he knew he couldn't continue without it.

Now it was almost dawn, and he was close. Close enough that he should be smelling her morning cookfire. But he smelled nothing.

As he rounded the last bend, he saw the footprints and stopped. White man's boots, two pairs, walking toward the pond . . . and in another wide spot, *one* man's footprints and the clear marks of White Bird's sandaled feet traveling away from the pond.

He dropped all his gear behind a group of

boulders. Taking only his knife, he crept along the boulders, avoiding the path. The man would be watching for him, and Coyote intended to surprise him from above.

Then he saw him. The white man sat on the rock by the pond, and next to him was his gun, his breakfast, and a long section of golden hair. *White Bird's hair.*

One man had taken her, one had stayed behind. Coyote considered his options carefully, and within seconds decided to conceal his knife under his loincloth and approach the man, hoping he would reveal if she was alive or already dead.

While the man stared up the path, Coyote jumped down from above and landed just behind the stranger.

The man whirled, then reached for his gun.

"Devious bastard!"

Coyote stood completely still, and waited.

"A few days late, aren't you?" Then he held up the section of braided hair, and an excited light filled his eyes. "Look familiar? My companion has taken her as insurance, just in case you might be thinking of backing out of the deal."

Coyote pointed to the hair, then out to the desert.

"Yes, she's safe and secure. Don't you speak English?" The man's eyes narrowed as he waited for a response.

Coyote simply pointed again to the hair.

"Fine. We shall go to her," he said, shaking

the braid. "At least for now, we need each other."

Coyote pointed to the cave, then the water, then cupped his hands as though to drink. Resisting the urge to question the man, his instincts told him it would be to his advantage if he was thought ignorant of the white man's language. He hoped when he reached White Bird, she would have already thought the same. Together, they might be able to plan her escape.

"Take whatever you need." The man nodded and pointed to the cave. "We'll leave as soon as you're ready, and when I've finished my breakfast."

The man laid his gun back on the rock, but kept his position so that he could watch. Casually, Coyote turned away to enter the cave. He packed a deerskin pouch with a few medicine bags, and the rest of the dried meat, then tied a full water gourd around his waist with some braided cord.

He was ready.

When he stepped outside the cave the man was waiting, and Coyote watched him reach into his pocket and pull out a black stone the size of a walnut. Then the man tossed it to him. Coyote caught the stone with one hand, and tossed it in the air to feel its weight. It was much heavier than the black rock he used for his arrow tips, and oddly shaped.

He tossed the stone back to the man.

"Good. I'm glad we understand each other. Who knows—I might choose to share some with you if there's as much gold as I think there is in those hills. You just need to take us there and your golden-haired squaw will be just fine." He tucked the piece of braid in his belt next to the gun, then nodded toward the trail and pointed to it. "You first."

Coyote walked three strides ahead of the man, memorizing the path as he went, filing away key landmarks in his mind. During the entire day, the man didn't speak, and Coyote was grateful for the silence. And when he was sure it would go unnoticed, he reached into his pouch to snatch pieces of meat. Too many days had passed without eating, and he knew he would need his strength for the fight to come.

"Hello, Mac!" the man suddenly called out.

Coyote had seen wisps of smoke from a small fire some time ago, and as the stranger shouted, the peaked roof of a wooden shack came into view.

Suzanne looked up, and when she saw Coyote her eyes stung with tears. She resisted the impulse to throw herself into his arms and cry with relief to see he was alive.

"Pete!" Mac shouted, dropping his empty bowl as he jumped up from his crouched position by the fire.

"Greetings, Mac, and say hello to our rather

mute and most reluctant guide. And *you*." He pointed a long finger at her. "Make us both something to eat."

She glanced at Coyote, and though she couldn't read his face, he moved his head from side to side in a barely perceptible motion. *Good*. She had hoped he had kept his knowledge of English hidden.

Coyote walked toward her, placed his supplies on the ground, then took a seat on a thick branch close to the fire while Mac and Pete disappeared into the wooden shack a few yards away.

She looked up, but he kept his gaze on the horizon.

"Are you hurt?" he whispered.

"I'm frightened."

"He had your hair."

"I'm fine."

"They think I will guide them to black stones of gold."

"Do you know what they're talking about?"

"I have heard of a white man, a man who walks with one leg—the other made of a wooden stick. This man found many black stones of gold, but could not find the same place again. Many white men have come to search for this place. Like these." His voice was hard with bitterness.

"What are we going to do?"

"I will help them, and think of how we can run away."

"Shhhh—they're coming."

Pete and Mac came out of the shed and sat

across from Coyote, their faces glowing with smiles. Pete reached for a bowl of food and a spoon. "Give him some."

Pete nodded toward Suzanne, and she filled a bowl for Coyote, then walked around the fire to hand it to him. He met her gaze, then stared at her face. His lips spread into a tight line and his eyes narrowed—his expression like what she guessed an animal's would be like as it prepared to kill its prey. He had definitely noticed her bruised cheek.

She shook her head a tiny bit, hoping he would control his reaction, then offered him a small smile to reassure him she was all right. His face had relaxed and was neutral by the time she returned to her seat.

"Miss, you'll need to interpret what I'm saying. Ask him where we can find more of these." He took a black stone out of his pocket and held it in the palm of his hand for her to see, then tossed it once more to Coyote.

Suzanne nodded at Pete, then reached for a stick.

"What are you doing?" Pete grabbed the stick out of her hand.

"I'll have to draw it out. It's the only way . . ."

She extended her hand, and Pete gave the stick back to her. With the bottom of her sandal, she smoothed out an area of sandy ground, then started to draw the shape of the hills in the distance, mimicking the horizon.

When she was finished, she pointed at the

black rock Coyote held, then pointed off in the distance and finally to the sketch in the sand. Glancing toward Pete, she explained out loud more for Coyote's sake than his. "I think he'll be able to figure out that this is the surrounding area, and he can indicate where he's going to take you. Here," she said as she handed the stick to Coyote, then nodded toward the ground.

He looked at the horizon, then her map, and then began to draw new hills and a horizon beyond hers. When he'd finished, he drew two suns off to the side, then tossed the black stone back to Pete.

"Well," she began as she examined his additions, "it looks as though your destination is actually beyond this ridge, a two-day walk from here." When she glanced at Coyote, she saw his barely perceptible affirmative nod.

"Excellent," Pete responded. "Mac, escort our guests to the shack for the night—you and I will bed down by the fire and get our supplies ready for our journey. We'll leave in the morning. Tell him." He pointed at her and waited.

Suzanne patted her chest, then pointed to Coyote, and finally to the structure. Coyote nodded and followed her toward the shack and into the doorway. The door slammed with a dull thud behind them, and she could hear it being barricaded with what sounded like at least two large boards.

Standing with her hands on her hips, she

looked around. The floor was hard-packed sand;
in the corner was a three-legged stool and a couple of blankets, and an empty tin bucket. Each
of the four walls contained a small opening
about a square foot in size that served as a window. The boards that made up the walls were
weathered silvery gray, and far from air-tight;
large gaps let in the fading light and a good
amount of circulation.

When the men's voices were faint enough to
indicate they'd returned to their seats by the fire,
Coyote pulled Suzanne to him.

They held each other for a long time before
either of them spoke.

"I had gone to the main trail," she explained,
"to meet you on the fifth day, and they were
waiting at the cave when I came back." Her voice
caught in her throat as she began to tell him
what had happened.

"How long here?"

"We've been here two days. I tried to tell them
I was alone, but they wouldn't believe me." Her
voice finally broke, and as she bit her lower lip
to keep herself from sobbing, he pulled her
closer and stroked her hair.

His touch satisfied her hunger for him, and
she tried to let herself get lost in the comfort of
his embrace. Finally, she relaxed in his arms.
They kept their silence for a while, and then Coyote pulled away.

He went to the corner where the blankets were

and brought them to his nose, then inspected them. He shook both out, then folded them into a pallet on the floor.

He sat, then gestured for her to join him. They reclined side by side, leaning their backs against the wall.

"Which one hit you?"

"Pete, the one with no hair on his face. It's fine—doesn't hurt at all."

Coyote sat silently. Unable to clearly read him in the fading light, Suzanne waited.

"These men," he began, "think I know this place, so I will take them."

"Where?"

The crunch of footsteps silenced them both as the men walked near enough to the cabin that their low voices were audible. Suzanne cupped her ear and strained to hear, picking up snatches of conversation as Pete and Mac got closer.

"Do you think he really . . ."

". . . and I don't trust him enough to . . ."

"So, what about the . . ."

". . . and we'll leave the woman here as insurance, so he won't be tempted to take us on a wild goose chase."

"What about *him*?"

"Well, we'll have her tell him we'll release him after he's shown us the gold, so he can come back for her. But . . ."

She couldn't hear the rest. Fearing the worst, she looked into Coyote's eyes to see if he'd understood. By the anger that flashed there, he had.

"I will take these men to the hills," he began again. It was clear they weren't coming back. "At the end of the first day, I will make tea that will make them sick. Too sick to follow me. And I will come for you. Then you must go to where white people can take you in, and I will go to my village."

"Why can't I go with—" He silenced any more words, putting his finger to her lips, then traced the perimeter of the black-and-blue stain on her cheek.

"I must go to my people. Then, after two moons, if you still wish to come to my village, I will come for you."

"Promise me?" She felt the sting of tears in her eyes, and fear knotted inside her.

He moved his hand to lift her chin. She looked for answers in his eyes, those black eyes that seemed to probe her very soul as he returned her gaze.

"You are *here*, White Bird," he said as he found her hand and placed it on his bare chest. "Put my words in your heart."

With a deep sigh, she closed her eyes and leaned into him, and they became still, arms wrapped around each other. They held each other tightly as the last of the evening light faded.

Her eyes fluttered open, and for a moment Suzanne couldn't quite decide where she was, but then she felt the slow rise and fall of Coyote's chest under her arm and she listened to the sound of his breathing. They must have both fallen asleep.

As she closed her eyes again, she thought about his decision to take her to the city, and tried to imagine herself in a nineteenth-century San Diego community. *Only temporarily, until he comes for me*, she reminded herself. She felt him begin to stir, and shifted a little so he could stretch his arms.

"Sleep?" he asked.

Before she could answer him, he moved his mouth over hers in a delicate, light kiss. She quivered at his tenderness, and pulled him closer so she could extend his kiss and drink in the sweetness. Gently, he pulled away, then kissed around her lips, her chin, and finally her bruised cheek. Her body tingled as his mouth descended, and he planted a tantalizing kiss in the hollow of her neck, then lay his head on her breast.

"I've missed you." Her voice came out in a broken whisper.

"My heart is glad you are here," he said.

She held him close, running her fingers through his hair and down his back.

"Will you tell me about your quest? Did everything turn out the way you expected?" He didn't answer immediately, and she wondered if she had been wrong to ask.

"I have seen many strange things—I do not know the words to use."

"Then I'll wait until your English is better, or my *Kumeyaay* improves," she said, and wrapped both arms around him.

"It is my dreams I want to tell you now. Before I was a full-grown man, many times I dreamed of a white bird. And then this white bird became a white woman. I was angry, but Grandfather told me I would meet her and my purpose was to protect her. You are my white bird."

Hearing him speak of his own recurring dreams made her feel as though things might finally be falling into place. Missing puzzle pieces found, a picture forming at last. Though the logic of it was still baffling, she began to sense the future just might supply the answers to questions she'd had since she was a girl. Questions she had never really been able to put into words.

"Your dreams and my dreams . . . they are one," he explained.

"I don't understand."

"When you sleep, you are here—here with Grandfather and with Coyote. When you sleep now, you dream of your home?"

"Yes." It was true. She hadn't had a desert dream since her first night at the oasis. Any dreams she'd remembered had always been of the life she'd left behind, life in the modern world—even, sometimes, pictures of a life to come, her possible future within what she now began to think of as her other world.

He lifted his head from her breast and looked into her eyes. "I will think of more good words, and we will talk of this again."

"It's morning. You'll be leaving soon." She could see the rays of a pink morning sun beginning to filter through the gaps in the walls.

"I will come for you, White Bird."

The approaching crunch of footsteps prevented her from responding to his words, but she felt elated by his promise and drew in a deep breath. And she knew in that moment, that instant, her heart belonged to him. They would have much to talk about and decisions to make when they were together again.

"Wake up in there!"

The sound of a fist banged against the door sent them both to their feet; then the door swung open and immediately caused her to shield her eyes against the light.

Pete entered the shack, his gun drawn. "Mac, bring in those things," he called over his shoulder. In a moment, Mac came in and set down a wooden crate. He handed Coyote his water gourd and supply pouch.

"You'll carry your own supplies and water," Pete said, pointing at Coyote's possessions.

Then Mac took from the crate a length of iron chain, and two padlocks.

"What are you going to do with that?" Suzanne asked, staring at the irons.

"Just a little added security," Pete replied.

Mac walked toward one of the far walls where he locked one end of the chain to an iron ring that must have been attached to something sunk into the ground. She hadn't even noticed it in the darkened corner.

She returned her gaze to Pete's gun, and hoped Coyote would remain calm. "Mind if I relieve myself before you lock me up?"

Pete nodded toward the empty tin bucket. "That will have to do for the next four days." Then he gestured for her to come closer.

Suzanne glared up at him and remained where she stood.

"There's food and water in the crate, and lucky for you it's not been too hot—you'll be just fine in here until we get back. Once we've seen the gold, we'll return, set you free, and we'll catch the Vallecito stage and go stake our claim. I made a deal, and all I expect is what I paid for."

Mac approached her and squatted so he could loop the chain around her ankle; then he attached and locked the padlock and gave it a firm tug.

She bit her lip to prevent herself from crying out. She didn't look at Coyote, but she hoped he'd noticed Mac had slipped the keys to the locks into his back pocket.

"Tell him it's time to go," Pete said, nodding toward Coyote.

Suzanne shifted her gaze to meet Coyote's darkened stare. *I'll be fine here. Don't worry—just come back when you can.* She forced a confident smile, and waited until his eyes brightened and the corners of his lips turned up just a tiny bit. Then she pointed at him and out the door.

# Chapter Fourteen

Coyote led the way at a fast enough pace the two men had to work hard to keep up with him. A destination firmly planted in his mind, he wanted to get as far as possible before they stopped for the night.

No one spoke until the sun blazed overhead and Mac whined enough that Pete agreed to a short break for water and lunch. Coyote declined the rations he was offered and waited, squatting near enough to hear their conversation.

"You think she'll be all right in the shack?" Mac asked. He chewed on some jerky and sipped water out of a metal cup as he crouched in the mottled shade of a large ocotillo.

"The days have been mild and the breeze was picking up when we left," Pete replied, "so she'll be comfortable enough until we return."

"You think he's really gonna take us to the gold?"

"The woman is probably valuable property for

him. I don't think he'll risk anything. Either way, we'll know his fate and ours tomorrow."

Mac belched loudly, then repacked his cup in the pouch of supplies he was carrying. Coyote stood, anxious to continue.

They walked until darkness fell, and Coyote pointed to a stand of boulders.

"I agree," Pete said. "That looks like a fine place to stop. Mac, gather some firewood."

Coyote dropped his gear and sat on a flat rock. Mac returned in a few minutes with an armload of dry branches and made a fire. As the man began to dig out pots and food supplies, Coyote stood and brought his own pouch of supplies to the campfire.

"What do *you* want?" Mac asked.

Coyote patted his chest and pointed to his pouch and then the fire.

"It seems our guide would like to prepare our dinner, Mac, and I for one would prefer something other than your usual burned slapjacks and miserable coffee. Let him cook."

Mac handed him the food sack, and Coyote looked through it to see if there might be anything he could use to supplement his own supplies. Inside he found white man's flour, some kind of putrid jerked meat, and a few other foodstuffs he didn't recognize. He set the bag aside and reached for his own, and quickly prepared a pot of acorn mush. When the mush was almost ready, he added some large pieces of dried rabbit, a pinch of salt, and some pine nuts.

Next he made a tea of dried plant stems and added some precious dried berries to make the flavor especially sweet. After it had steeped, he finally stirred in the jimsonweed. He tasted the tea, and the bitterness of the poisonous plant was undetectable.

When his preparation was complete, he served the two men with his head lowered and his gaze on the ground, adopting the demeanor the two expected of him.

"Well, aren't you going to have some?" Mac asked, his mouth so full he spit out some of the mush.

Pete hardly looked from his own bowl as he tossed an empty dish and cup to Coyote. "Eat. And pour us all some of that tea." He pointed to the pot.

Coyote scooped a bowl of mush, then poured the cooled tea into three tin cups. He ate his own meal quickly.

He'd ingested small amounts of *tolvaach* during most of his life to build up a tolerance; what he'd put into the drink would have no effect on him. He guessed it would be only minutes before the men would be doubled over, their stomachs reacting violently to the toxic plant.

Both men asked for more tea, and Coyote obliged. He observed them from his position on the rock, first noticing Mac's eyebrows pull together in an agonized expression, surprise coloring his face. Then Pete rubbed his stomach as his mouth took on an unpleasant twist, awareness slowly creeping into his expression.

"What have you done?" Pete gasped from the sharp pain, his hand fumbling at his belt for his gun. Shock and amazement came next, then suddenly his face went grim.

Coyote smiled. Pete had forgotten he'd put his gun on the ground several feet away when he'd inspected their food supplies . . . just as hoped.

Mac rolled forward as he clutched his abdomen while Pete struggled to remain erect, his arms wrapped tightly around his lower half. His face was twisted with loathing, and Coyote could see the sheen of sweat on the man's forehead.

When he was certain both men were unable to defend themselves, he approached Mac who was still writhing on the ground, and deftly pulled the two padlock keys from his back pocket. Then he began to gather his supplies, tying his half-full water gourd around his waist.

"You've killed us," Pete said in a harsh, raw voice.

Coyote stopped and shook his head. "You will not die. When the sun is high in the sky tomorrow, you will no longer feel the pain of *tolvaach.*"

"But the gold—," Mac whined.

"I know not the place of the heavy black stones."

"You deceitful, insidious—"

Pete's words were interrupted by a long, gut-wrenching groan, and Coyote turned his back on both men and began to run.

\* \* \*

*Grandfather?*

*I am here Coyote.*

*I have many questions.*

*What have you learned, grandson?*

*I know I am to learn the ways of the* kuseyaay *from you. I know this is what I will become and, above all else, I know I must return to our people.*

*And what confuses you?*

*In my night dream, there was clear danger for me in returning to White Bird.*

*But you returned.*

*And the dream was right. I am afraid I have chosen wrong, my grandfather, and my people are now in danger.*

*Do not worry of your people now, grandson, for I have breath still in me and I am watching over them. We have a long journey to take, you and I, but you must first follow your heart. Go to the white woman, for you must still protect her.*

*Where will I find you?*

*We will be together, Hattepaa, when the moon is new, in our village in the mountains.*

Coyote stopped to rest for just a few minutes, and to drink the last of his water. First light would come soon and he knew he was close.

His running had become a prayer—a prayer for his people, a prayer for White Bird's safety, a prayer he would learn well from his grandfather.

Over and over he considered his options while

he ran, and though his future was far from certain, he knew clearly that his path was to become the last shaman of his people. But would they accept White Bird if she chose to come with him?

Life for her would be difficult with so much to learn—would she choose to leave her own kind forever? She had surprised him in how much she had already mastered in the short time they'd been together, and she seemed suited to the ways of his people. But would she be content to always be on the run? Always moving, always following the food source, avoiding the impact of the white man?

It would be her decision, and he had experienced firsthand the strength of her determination, her resolve.

White Bird. His teacher and his apprentice.

He wondered if Grandfather had known all along. Perhaps he had ridden the wind to already see this moment, this instant when his life would take its new course. No, Grandfather would simply shake his head and scold him for thinking this. "Life is a journey for all people," he would say, "with many paths to seek, many paths to find."

Coyote finally rose, and began to run again. The horizon he focused on grew hazy, and it wasn't long before he realized he was running toward a sand-filled sky.

He had seen other storms when the sand flew through the air so violently that all living creatures took shelter until it returned to its place on the desert floor.

The way grew more and more difficult, the sand whirling around him, stinging his skin as though a thousand tiny claws nipped at him. He pushed forward at a walk now, looking for larger landmarks when the path disappeared altogether in the swirling sand.

At last he thought he saw the shack in the distance, but when he shouted, the storm swallowed his words. He could barely make out the silhouette of the building, and what he could see blurred as he walked closer, leaning hard against the biting wind.

Pounding on the door with both fists, he called to Suzanne, then pulled away the heavy boards the men had used to barricade it. He tugged the handle toward him, using the last of his strength, but the wind fought his efforts as it pushed against the door.

"*White Bird*!" He called her name over and over, though he feared she wouldn't hear him over the roar of the wind.

The door opened a crack, and he used one of the boards to lever it open, finally freeing it enough so the wind helped swing it open.

A stinging cloud of sand rushed in with the wind as he entered the shack. He felt with his hands for the chain, following it link by link until he reached the other end. It was still padlocked in a small loop where Pete had placed it around her ankle. Both the chain and the padlock were whole and uncut, but White Bird was gone.

# Chapter Fifteen

Suzanne's eyes felt like they were filled with thick glue as she struggled to blink them open. But she couldn't quite wake up, caught as she was in that place between wakefulness and sleep. Her thoughts were a jumble of confused images, and she tried to translate them into something more concrete.

It must be morning. But where was Coyote?

The sound of the wind had grown through the night, the constant pinging of sand against the wood of the shack kept her from sleeping—*that*, she remembered. And sometime in the middle of the night, the sand started blowing through the window-holes and the many cracks in the walls until she'd taken one of the blankets and pulled it over her head. She'd curled into a ball, hiding from the angry storm, hoping the weather had been better for Coyote as he'd led the men away from the shack.

She'd prayed his plan would work and then

almost laughed at the thought that she had anything to fear. Of course his plan would work, and he would be back by daybreak.

*Morning. Where was he?*

She sat up, a wave of dizziness hitting her from the sudden movement. She lay back down and counted to twenty, then tried again. This time it was better and she stretched her arms, finally rubbing the sleep from her eyes.

*Morning.* She was sure it was morning, but the light was dim. One thing was certain, she was elated to have survived the night in one piece. She adjusted her top and tugged at her jeans, then stopped, her fingers tingling against the denim.

*What was I just thinking?*

*Morning.* But there had been something else. The remnants of any other thoughts dissolved as she came fully awake and looked out the cave's entrance, popping the last of her Tic Tacs into her mouth. She stretched her neck to work out the kinks, again berating herself for not grabbing her daypack before she'd left on her hike. If she had, she could be drinking a nice cup of purified water right about now, plus eating a tasty lemon protein bar for breakfast. *And* she could have popped a couple of aspirin to help with this pounding headache.

Other than the throbbing in her head, she felt fine. In fact, she felt wonderful, amazed she had come through the earthquake without a serious injury. Her eyebrows drew together in a frown as she ran her hand up and down her left arm, sure she should at the very least be feeling a scrape or two. She was positive there *had* been injuries. How could she have healed so quickly?

She shook away the jumble of confused thoughts and exited the cave. Outside, she dipped her bandanna into the pond and wiped her face and arms, the morning air a cool breath against her damp skin. The water was still and inviting, but she resisted the urge to wiggle out of her clothes for a quick dip before she headed toward the trailhead.

*It would be just my luck to be caught skinny-dipping as my rescuers arrive.*

Dropping down to sit on a flat rock close to the shore, she gazed at the mirrorlike surface of the water. The air filled her lungs and, with each breath, she felt more and more alert. Her stomach added its grumble, and she stood up and began a few stretches.

As she finished her leg lunges, a sound on the other side of the pond interrupted her focus, and when she turned her head to pinpoint the rustling, a coyote stepped into view. His stare never left her as he walked slowly toward the water's edge.

"Thirsty?" she whispered. He looked exhausted, as though he'd walked many miles to find the watering hole. To him, it was a life-giving miracle in the harsh desert. He seemed harmless, and she didn't have the heart to clap her hands and try to shoo him away.

"Plenty of room for the both of us, friend." She watched as he drank his fill, delicately lapping at the water. When he'd finished, he sat on his haunches, watching her intently. His expression was not aggressive in any way; it actually seemed almost sad, and she began to wonder if the animal was ill.

"It's a beautiful morning and I'd love to stay here with you, but I really have to go." She stood up and dusted off the back of her jeans. When she took one last look across the pond, the coyote had disappeared.

The buzz of the helicopter was the first sound of civilization she heard, and the aircraft swooped low, sending lizards darting across her path, scampering away from the infernal monster. She waved a one-handed greeting, and hoped they could see she was all right.

The trail was in pretty poor shape, much of it covered with debris and rocks, some so large she had to clamber over or around them to get back on what little of the path she could identify. There would be many hours of volunteer cleanup ahead to return the trail to its original condition. Perhaps she could bring some students out before she left town.

Her stomach tightened, not out of hunger this time, but from something else. But what that something else was, she hadn't a clue. She concentrated, looking for an explanation.

It wasn't the job offer. She'd worked everything out before she'd fallen asleep. The university was offering the opportunity of a lifetime, and she would take the position. Her plan was to negotiate as much vacation and sabbatical time as she could so she could spend her off-hours in this desert park. It would be easy to justify. There would be research needed for journal articles, new curriculum to be developed, lectures to prepare. She could write a damn textbook if they wanted her to. It would work out just fine.

No, there was something else tugging at her heart and making her stomach sour, something else that drew her eyebrows together in a deep frown and kept causing her to stop and look over her shoulder, back to where she'd come from.

"Hey! Someone's coming off the trail!" someone shouted.

She lifted her hand toward a group of emergency personnel gathered beneath a white canopy near the restroom and shower building. If the water pumps were still working, she'd have at least a lukewarm shower to look forward to.

There were several tents set up, and another white canopy where some Red Cross staff were seated at tables, plus several green-capped Park Rangers walking around. She decided to check in with the Red Cross and let them know she wasn't hurt, just tired and dusty.

"Hi, I'm Suzanne Lucas. I was camping here—"

One of the rangers handed her a cell phone. "You're first on my list, and you're to call someone named Robin and let her know you're all right."

Suzanne punched in Robin's number and held the phone to her ear, then walked a few yards in the opposite direction from the local news van she'd spotted. One of the popular local news anchors stood next to a huge displaced boulder that had rolled onto a Lexus SUV. He appeared to be interviewing the vehicle's owner, probably going for an up-close-and-personal look at the damage from the earthquake, just in time for the noon newscast.

She kept her face turned away; the last thing she wanted to do at that moment was be questioned by a reporter. Besides, there would be dozens of geologists and seismic specialists around who could provide plenty of on-air analysis and sound bites.

She just wanted to go home.

After several rings, Robin's machine picked up.

"You've reached my machine, so leave a message. If this is you, Suze, let me know if you're okay."

She smiled at the personal greeting her friend had added, and waited for the beep. "Robin, it's Suzanne. I'm not hurt—I spent the night at the Palm Canyon oasis and just walked out this morning. Why don't we get together tomorrow, okay?" She paused for a second, then added,

"And I'm taking the job, by the way. See you soon. Bye."

Keeping her back toward any cameras she could see, Suzanne returned to the Red Cross tent to turn in the phone. A gray-haired woman, whose weathered and lined face indicated she was no stranger to the desert sun, gestured for her to have a seat across from her. The woman reached for a brown clipboard, and put it on the table between them. A pen dangled by a string, and the woman pulled it up and grasped it tightly. She was all business, and Suzanne waited for instructions.

"Name?"

"Suzanne Lucas. I was camping here and got caught down by the palms when the earthquake hit."

The woman nodded, and scribbled onto the form, then asked for her address and phone number. "How do you feel? Any injuries to report?"

"Nope, I'm fine."

"Go over to the next tent. They'll check your vitals."

"Like I said, I'm fine."

The woman glanced up from her clipboard and glared, then her eyes took on a quizzical expression.

"I know, I must look a mess," Suzanne said as she patted her wild curls. "Are the showers working?"

The woman paused for a split second before

nodding, then licked her thumb and pulled off the top copy of the form. She handed it to Suzanne, then pointed at the tent.

At the medical tent, the only thing Suzanne asked for was some aspirin. The headache had worsened since she'd arrived at the organized chaos of the rescue operation. Everything seemed a little too frenetic and a lot too loud.

The staff seemed relieved she hadn't been hurt and shared with her that no serious injuries had been reported so far. After she filled out the last form, they released her to go back to her campsite.

Her green Honda CR-V was right where she'd parked it next to her tent. The campsite looked untouched, a thick layer of dust the only sign that the earthquake had even occurred.

She zipped open the tent door and reached for a clean set of clothes, a towel, and her cosmetic bag. The showers were calling her name.

The water was barely lukewarm, but it didn't matter. Closing her eyes, she felt each of her muscles relax. Standing in the steady stream of water, she quieted her mind and tried to think of nothing except how her skin tingled and how good it felt to breathe in the moist air. The sound of the water against the concrete walls and floor became almost like a meditation; and behind her closed eyes, pictures flashed.

*Palm Canyon. The cave. Cooking over a fire?* Was she remembering snatches of long-forgotten dreams? Somehow, she didn't think so. Then blurred visions of a man surfaced, one with long black hair and wonderful, expressive eyes. He must be her dream man, but in her dreams she'd never been able to remember his face. This was different. This was new. His black eyes stared directly at hers, eyes filled with first anger and then sorrow. And in every instance and from every angle, as she pictured him, his hand beckoned her to go with him. *Who are you?*

Then fear, stark and vivid, glittered in his dark eyes. Panic like she'd never known before welled in her throat, and she choked back a frightened cry. A cold knot formed in her stomach and she breathed in shallow quick gasps as she desperately held on to the vision of his face.

He was real . . . she was certain of it.

The sound of women's voices jarred her, and in an instant the face vanished, and she was unable to retrieve it. Every time she tried, all she could remember was the expression in his dark eyes. For the moment, he was gone, and all she could do was hope she might see him again when she slept.

The women's chattering grew louder as she realized they were waiting in line for a shower stall. Breathing out a heavy sigh, she reluctantly ended her indulgence, dried off, and slipped into shorts and a tee shirt, balling up her dirty clothes to take back with her.

It was crowded in front of the mirrors, and she waited for an opening at one of the sinks and

Janet Wellington

scooted into place just as a Red Cross volunteer finished. She'd super conditioned her hair at the end of her shower, and ran her fingers through it, then pulled a widetoothed comb through until her curls were tangle-free.

As she wiped the condensation from the mirror and looked at herself, she took a quick breath of utter astonishment. Running parallel about an inch below her hairline was a thick black wavy line. She tried rubbing it with her fingertips, but it remained. Her heart pounded as she lathered up a washcloth, scrubbed her face as hard as she could, then rinsed and looked again. Her skin glowed pink, but the mark remained. She traced the line with an index finger. It wasn't a scratch—but what *was* it?

Taking her comb, she re-parted her hair low on one side so she could sweep it over the mark and secure the ends behind her ear. Satisfied she looked reasonably normal, she turned to leave.

No one reacted, and she assumed anyone who might have seen the mark had thought what she had: that it was a dirty scratch gotten somehow in the mayhem of the earthquake.

She froze in mid-stride on the path back to her tent as a new thought formed. *A tattoo?* That could be one reason for her throbbing headache, but there was absolutely no logic she could apply to the fact that she'd woken up with an indelible mark on her forehead that, if it *was* a tattoo, had been purposely and skillfully applied.

212

There hadn't been time, for one thing. *Time.* That was the other thing that was bothering her. She knew she'd had injuries before she'd fallen asleep in the cave the night before. She ran her fingers along her left arm, only feeling the slightly raised skin of well-healed scars.

And she had a strange feeling she'd been gone, really gone, for more than one night. More unexplained sensations.

Resuming her walk she quickened her pace, determined to break camp and head for home as quickly as she possibly could.

Coyote hadn't really believed he would find White Bird at the pond, but he returned there anyway. He found the rest of his things in the cave, undisturbed and untouched. There was no sign of her.

In fact, it was as though she'd never been there. Only one sleeping blanket was laid out. Even the deerskin she'd used to wrap around herself was now folded neatly on top of one of his pouches. One bowl and spoon lay next to the fire pit. One drinking bowl. Even the smell of her was gone.

Her absence made his heart cold and still, and the normally comfortable peacefulness of the cave became instead a chilly black silence. He felt an acute sense of loss and grief, and despair tore at his heart.

Had he lost her completely? Was she waiting somewhere he could go?

*Grandfather!*

There was no reply, only his own tormented moan. Stumbling outside, he dropped to his knees at the shoreline and splashed water on his face. If this was a dream, he wished to awaken.

Instead, the swell of regret filled him. If he hadn't left her for his vision quest, they would have avoided the wealth-seekers and she would be safe . . . with him. Guilt replaced regret.

But if he hadn't left her, he might never have had the visions he'd had, his path revealed. All things were dependent on other things; many times his grandfather had taught him so.

This lesson, though, seemed meaningless and wrong.

In his mind he reviewed every memory of her until he could capture each day's mood or achievement or joy, until he was sure no moment would ever be forgotten. He remembered . . . until White Bird was etched in his mind forever, safe and secure.

As the light dimmed and the creatures came to the pond, he watched an owl glide over the water, landing on a nearby branch.

A message?

As he stared at the owl, before his eyes its form began to undulate until it finally blurred and transformed into a glow of light. Shielding his eyes, he kept his gaze on the spot as the light began to take on a new shape. As the silhouette began to take a more solid form, he realized he now looked upon the white bird of his dreams.

And a cry of relief broke from his lips.

*Grandfather. I am coming.*

He gathered his supplies and prepared himself for the long journey to his people's summer home. There he would be an apprentice . . . and there he would learn how to bring White Bird back.

# Chapter Sixteen

When Suzanne's eyes blinked open, she was sitting up with her arms reaching out, her mouth open in a silent scream. She brought her hands to her cheeks to wipe away the tears, her chest still heaving with sobs.

Shoving aside the bedspread, she almost fell from the bed as she rushed to the bathroom. With only the soft glow of the nightlight, she opened a drawer and pulled out a pair of shears and began cutting her hair.

Tears blinded her eyes as she wept aloud. Grasping handfuls of hair, she continued to cut. Long strands fell into the sink while flashes of wild grief ripped through her. As she stared into the mirror, she saw his face instead of her own, and torment squeezed her heart. When she'd finished, she stumbled back to bed and collapsed face down so that her sobs were muffled by the pillow.

\* \* \*

It couldn't be thundering. Suzanne rolled over onto her side to look at the clock on her nightstand. *Ten after two.* Forcing her eyes more open, she realized the daylight streaming through her window meant it was P.M., not A.M. She'd slept through the night and well into the next day.

The pounding noise resumed, and her brain finally connected. Someone was at the door.

"I'm coming—," she called out.

"Suze, it's Robin!"

She glanced down and realized she'd slept in her clothes, and that she hardly even remembered the drive home from the desert. She must have simply fallen into bed when she'd arrived.

As she made her way to the door, she rubbed her eyes to force them to stay open. She felt drugged, and walked slowly so she could re-orient herself. She unlocked the door and opened it, the bright sunlight forcing her eyes closed again. She felt herself being pulled into a firm hug, then pushed away and held at arm's length.

"Jeez—what *happened* to you?" Robin asked.

Suzanne opened her eyes a crack and gave her friend a weak smile. "Please tell me you brought coffee."

In a graceful movement, Robin pivoted and bent over to pick up two paper bags sitting on the front stoop. "Better than that, my friend—I brought pastries and two mochas."

"You, are my personal savior."

They walked into the kitchen and Robin promptly pushed Suzanne into a chair, her hand solid on her shoulder. "You sit and relax." Then she pulled a plate out of the cupboard and returned to the table. She opened one bag to retrieve two large paper cups, then opened the other bag and put the pastries on the plate.

Suzanne's mouth began to water; she couldn't remember her last meal.

"Cranberry scone," Robin said, pointing at the plate. "Apple turnover, cheese danish, and a double-fudge brownie, just in case."

Suzanne reached for the scone and a napkin, while Robin scooted one of the cups toward her.

"I got your voice message," Robin began, "but you didn't mention your hair."

Suzanne wrinkled her forehead as she chewed, then took a sip from the steaming cup before she answered. "What?"

"I can probably fix that—even out the bangs and trim the sides back to one length."

Suzanne lifted her hands to her head and began to feel her hair. "Oh, my *God!*" She sprang from her chair and raced to the bathroom. Staring at her image in the mirror, a tumble of confused thoughts and feelings swept through her. Then she looked down at the sink where she saw a tangled pile of long pieces of golden, wavy hair.

She felt her friend's hand on her shoulder, and allowed Robin to guide her back to the kitchen and push her into the chair.

"I don't know what happened," she whispered.

219

"Well, I guess it doesn't really matter. It's done. I'll fix it after you eat." Robin pointed at the scone in front of her.

Halfheartedly, Suzanne finished the scone and took a few more gulps of coffee.

"You ready to talk about it?" Robin asked, her voice soothing and gentle.

Suzanne stared into the face of her friend, whose expression was still and serious. "Don't look so worried, Robin. You're scaring me."

"I *am* worried. Something's happened to you."

"I know. The thing is, I can't remember much."

"You've had a shock—"

"No, it's not like that. I remember the earthquake, but I feel like I've been away a lot longer than the one night I spent at Palm Canyon."

"Tell me more."

"The scrapes I got from rocks falling during the earthquake have all healed, and I know I had a bad gash on my arm and my upper back. I remember that. Everything's healed."

Robin got up and pulled at the neck of Suzanne's tee shirt to check her shoulder. "All I see is a reddened area. You sure it was scraped and not just bruised?"

"Absolutely sure. That's what I'm saying. I'm in good shape, *too* good."

"What else?" Robin asked. She sat back in her chair.

Suzanne licked the crumbs off her fingertips, wiped her hand on a napkin, then lifted her new bangs. "This." She watched as Robin's eyes widened with concern. "I think it's a tattoo."

"It won't wash off?"

"Nope."

"Well, your new bangs cover it nicely."

"Always the silver lining . . ."

"Sorry, but it's pretty interesting, you know. Reminds me of that Sean Connery movie . . . the one in the rain forest where the woman ends up with a blue tattoo on her forehead."

Suzanne nodded. "But I can't remember, Robin, and it's killing me."

"Did you dream while you slept last night? Do you remember anything?"

Suzanne closed her eyes and took a deep breath. Immediately, vivid images of a man's face appeared, his black eyes shining with tenderness. "I can see his face now."

"Your dream man? Tell me."

"Black hair hanging free, well past his shoulders. Dark eyes. Bronzed skin, high cheekbones, strong nose and chin. And when he smiles at me, I melt. I'm worthless. Though it wasn't that way from the beginning. At first, he was aloof, and—"

"Wait," Robin interrupted. "What do you mean . . . from the beginning?"

Suzanne's eyes snapped open. She had heard her own words, and understood she had spoken as though she had gotten to know him . . . over time. "Robin, this is starting to feel really strange."

"Suze, think hard—are you talking about a dream, or a memory?"

"I know it doesn't make any sense, but I don't think it was from a dream."

They sat in silence for a few moments. "I have an idea," Robin said. "Why don't I stay with you today . . . and tonight. If you wake up, I'm right here and maybe your dreams will start giving us some clues."

Suzanne nodded. She didn't want to be alone, and her friend's company perhaps would fill the void she felt. There was an indescribable something that haunted her. Inside, she felt a bitterness and a loneliness that had to be coming from somewhere. She stifled a yawn, surprised she felt tired after her long sleep and the mocha.

Robin answered her question. "They were decaf, by the way, in case you were wondering. Why don't you bring me some scissors and a comb, and I'll try straightening out that haircut."

Suzanne smiled and rose from the table to retrieve the shears she'd seen on the bathroom counter, next to the sink.

In the bathroom, she scooped the hair out of the sink and into the wastebasket, then knelt on the floor beside the tub to hold her head under the faucet. After she'd blotted her wet hair, she grabbed the scissors, a comb, and a dry bath towel, carefully avoiding the mirror. When she returned to the kitchen, Robin had already pulled one of the chairs into the middle of the room.

"The salon is open," Robin said. She patted the back of the chair.

Suzanne handed her friend the shears and draped the towel over her own shoulders as she sat down. "You really think you can fix it?"

"Sure. You just relax," Robin replied. She started combing through the damp hair. "I'm going to trim it to one length, about even with your jaw line, then fringe the bangs a little so you can just fluff them."

As Robin worked her miracle, Suzanne relaxed, relishing the gentle touch of her friend's hands on her head and the fingers tugging at her hair while she snipped. Then a picture began to form behind her closed eyes, and she concentrated until it came into focus. She saw herself as though she were watching from above—she was lying on the ground, leaning backward, her head near the edge of a pond. It was the pond at Palm Canyon.

And Coyote was pouring water over her hair.

"Stop," Suzanne said, tipping her head and pulling her hair out of Robin's grasp.

"What?"

"This is weird, Robin, but now I really think somehow it was all real. I just remembered something . . . but not like it was a dream. Like it was real. His name is Coyote."

She felt Robin's hands on her shoulders. "*Is,* or *was*?"

"Is," Suzanne replied. "He's flesh and blood, Robin. I don't know how I know it, but I do."

"Okay," Robin said as she continued to snip. "Give me details."

"We were at the oasis, and he was washing my hair. But, it was like I was . . . *watching* myself."

"Like an out-of-body thing?"

"I guess. But it was so clear—nothing like my vague dream images. More like watching a movie, but I could *feel* everything that was happening. I felt the coolness of the water, the touch of his hands."

"Well, I'm guessing my hands on your head stimulated this—whatever it is—triggering some kind of cellular memory. You think?"

"I don't know. Sounds too far-out."

"It's all I'm coming up with. I'm not saying it makes sense, but try to keep an open mind."

"I'm not as willing as you are to believe things that can't be explained."

"Suzanne, take a look at the facts as you know them—as you *think* you know them. Major cuts and scrapes that have healed in twenty-four hours. A midnight-madness haircut that looks worse than if a four-year-old had done it. Vivid pictures that sound a heck of a lot more like memories than leftover dream images—"

"Okay, okay. You almost done?"

"With your haircut, but not the rest." She whipped the towel from Suzanne's shoulders and shook the curls onto the floor. "You go look and I'll sweep up."

Suzanne walked to the bathroom and looked

in the mirror. Her friend had indeed done wonders. "Why'd you ever stop doing hair, anyway? This looks great," she called out.

Robin leaned her head into the bathroom. "Not enough challenging clients like you. Actually, I think it suits you, Professor Lucas."

Suzanne patted her springy curls into place, then spritzed them with some spray gel. Examining her face in the mirror, she forced her lips into a stiff smile. She had a phone call to make.

"Well, what'd they say?" Robin asked as she reached for the brownie and divided it in two. "Want some?"

Suzanne put the cordless phone on the table and took the other half of the brownie. "They're delighted I called, and are expecting me two weeks before Labor Day."

"Don't look so excited," Robin teased.

"I'm pleased . . . really."

"Convince me."

"Of course I'll miss Southern California and school and the desert—but *you're* leaving anyway, so there's no one keeping me here. I keep reminding myself it's such a great job."

"They paying your moving expenses?"

Suzanne shook her head. "Not their policy," she said as she dialed another number.

"Who you calling now?"

"I'm checking my voicemail at school. There should be a message whether or not there were enough sign-ups for summer semester." While she listened, Robin wiped the crumbs from the table and wrapped up the remaining turnover and danish.

"By the frown on your face, I'm guessing bad news?" she asked.

"I'll have to look for something else to pad my savings account for the move."

"Maybe you'll have to put that minor in English to work, huh?"

"Maybe. Tomorrow I can check the job board in the faculty lounge and see what's left." Suzanne stifled a yawn as she looked around her kitchen, guessing how many moving boxes she'd need for that room alone.

"Hey, you want to watch a DVD? It'll be like a sleepover—you go pick something out and I'll make us some grilled-cheese sandwiches, now that we've already had our dessert."

Suzanne returned her friend's smile, then walked into the tiny living room that was more library than a place to entertain. Overflowing bookshelves lined each of the walls. They were filled with volumes she'd collected over the years. Most of them specialized in the flora and fauna of the desert regions, and now she'd be adding new ones, ones that would feature the trees and plants of the Pacific Northwest.

It would be exciting to learn along with the students. She loved developing new programs, and the greenhouse the dean had described sounded perfect for research projects. The well-supported private university offered a stimulating, intellectual challenge—a job with a future and long-term security. It was perfect. The best news she could hope to have.

Clearly, a good decision. *Where I won't know a soul and I'll be a thousand miles from home.* No, it would *become* her new home, she argued with herself. And the desert would always be there, waiting for her visits.

A feeling of isolation and separation washed through her in a cold wave. It was good not to be alone right now, she confirmed, and Robin would help keep her mind occupied for the next few hours with her neverending buoyant mood and nonstop chatter.

Shuffling through a stack of jewel cases, she spotted *Medicine Man*. Perfect. As Suzanne hit the play button, Robin came into the room and put a tray on the coffee table. On it were two gooey, grilled-cheese sandwiches, a basket of tortilla chips, and a bowl of salsa.

"Girlfriend—you are going to miss my cooking," Robin said, popping a chip into her mouth.

"No, I'm going to miss *you.*"

# Chapter Seventeen

"Good shawii."

Suzanne smiled as she felt the heat in her cheeks, a result of the loving sound in his voice. "You're easy to please." She handed Coyote her empty bowl and watched him wipe it out.

She had grown so used to his face, his touch, the rhythm of his breathing at night as they lay close together. It was difficult to remember what it was like without him. In his simple ways, he had taught her more than she'd learned with all her advanced education. This was the way life was supposed to be.

His eyes shone as he stepped toward her and pulled her into his arms, and they shared a deep, long kiss that made her weak in the knees and totally defenseless.

When their lips finally parted, he looked into her eyes. But instead of the affection she usually saw, there was a touch of sadness, and her mind began to whirl. Confusing emotions filled her and she felt frozen, unable to move or speak.

*"We will be together for more than these short moments. Look in your heart for my promise," he whispered.*

*She blinked, and now he stood several yards away, one hand extended. His expression was one of strength, and his eyes shone with a steadfast and serene peace. She blinked again, and he was almost out of sight. She wanted to shout to him, run to him. But she was paralyzed.*

*How could he look so determined when he was moving farther and farther away?*

*"Come back," she finally cried, her voice quavering. "Come back!"*

"Suze, wake up! It's a dream, it's a dream. . . ."

Suzanne opened her eyes wide to see Robin's face a few inches from her own.

"You were crying out so loud you woke me up in the other room. Close your eyes right now, and try to go back to the dream. I'll go get my notebook."

Suzanne obeyed, her eyelids fluttering closed. *Come back.* She felt Robin's weight on the edge of the bed, and then the flutter of pages being flipped.

"Okay, talk."

"Coyote and I were together. We had shared a meal and he took my bowl. I was thinking about how I had made the right decision—to stay with him, how I liked learning what he had to teach me more than what I had spent my whole educational career learning. And then he

was . . . kissing me. And then he was so, so sad—
I can't remember why. But then he said to look
for . . . his promise . . . in my heart. But I can't remember what it is, what he promised me." Her
words ended in a sob as frustration over-
whelmed her reasoning.

"It's okay, it's okay," Robin whispered.

"None of this makes sense to me, Robin!"

"And that's bothering you more than anything
else, I know."

"It's different now . . ."

"You remembered a lot, now sit up and dry
your eyes—you want some water?"

Suzanne sat up and reached for a tissue to
wipe her face, then drank the glass of water
Robin offered. "No, I mean it's different because
I feel like I was really, really there."

"Because . . ." Robin encouraged.

"I had real thoughts. Thoughts about my real
life . . . *this* life . . . you know?"

"Suze. I've recorded everything you've ever
told me about your dreams in this journal. Tomorrow, let's go over some of them. Maybe we
can come up with, I don't know, a kind of history or timeline or something."

It sounded logical, like a good idea. Suzanne
nodded, and squeezed her friend's hand. "Promise me right now that we'll talk to each other at
least once a week, no matter what."

"Or more if it's good news," Robin agreed.
"Hey, I'm counting on going to the Tony Awards
next year if all goes well with my guy's career.

I'll be calling you often to read all the rave theater reviews—and to tell you what I'm wearing to the big show."

Suzanne smiled at the enthusiasm and adoration she saw in her friend's eyes. "You are *so* in love, aren't you?"

"Oh, yeah. This is the guy, Suze."

"You deserve it."

"And so do you—don't be so convinced you're going to be married to your career forever. Things happen. And things have a way of sneaking up on you—you just have to really, really want it, sometimes."

"And be open."

"And be open," Robin agreed.

"I'm going back to sleep, Miss Merry Sunshine."

"Okay. If I'm not here when you wake up, I've gone to meet my true love for a jog around campus, okay?"

"Goodnight."

Suzanne stared at the ceiling for what seemed like hours, finally hearing the rustle of movement in the living room just as the first rays of morning crept past her drawn curtains. Then she heard the soft closing of the front door as Robin went to jog.

Throwing off the covers, she headed for the bathroom for a hot shower. The minute Robin returned, she planned to check what job opportunities remained for the rest of the summer. She

only had two months to earn the cash she'd need
in order to move.

It felt good to have a new goal, something that
would take her mind off the unexplainable. She
craved the comfort that the structure of a summer job would provide even more than the fi-
nancial boost it would give her.

In the faculty lounge, Suzanne ran her finger
down the list of positions and code numbers,
and jotted down the best prospects onto a scrap
of paper. She waited for one of the computer ter-
minals to free up, then went to the school's in-
tranet page and keyed in her password.

She clicked on the JOBS button and searched
on the first code number to check its status.
"Well, that one's filled," she muttered. She
worked her way down the list, but found each
position either filled or unconfirmed because of
funding delays.

She held her breath as she keyed in her last
code number and waited for the information to
appear. The position description filled the
screen. At least it was open and applications
were being accepted.

Individualized tutoring with elementary
school students, all subjects; English degree
a plus. Two-hour sessions will take place on
campus, utilizing the library study rooms.
Hours: 8–5, through August 15th. Salary

commensurate with experience and degree
qualifications.

Hours were good, timing was perfect. She jotted down the number and dialed it from the
phone on the wall above the monitor.

After a brief conversation and an online con-
firmation of her credentials, she had the job. And
she could start in the morning. She'd have only
three students, all of whom needed help with
reading and composition. She'd also have the
added luxury of paid prep time.

*Piece of cake*, she thought as she strolled back
to her apartment. Another perfect job at the perfect time. Things were beginning to fall into
place. A sense of strength came to her, and the
despair she had been feeling began to lessen. It
would be a good thing, she knew, and would fill
her days in a productive way—plus she would
earn just enough to comfortably cover all her
moving expenses.

Life, again, was good. Almost.

Suzanne stared at the empty chair across from
her, and drummed her fingers on the table. Her
second student was a no-show ... again. And
when she glanced through the glass walls of the
study room, she could see Hector was early ...
again. He had explained to her the first day she
shouldn't worry about it. Though it took him a
couple of hours to come the forty miles on the
bus that ran from the Barona reservation to the

college, he never complained and was always prepared for their session. He was a kid eager to please.

And here they both sat, she inside the study room and Hector in one of the hard chairs outside the room.

"This is silly," she said out loud. She would just take him early. She got up and poked her head out the doorway, and gestured for him to come into the room.

"Hector, why don't we go ahead and start, okay?"

He shrugged; then his perpetual smile widened in approval. He'd learned well and quickly over the last six weeks. She liked him, and not just because he was a model student. More than once she'd wondered why he was in the intervention program at all. She assumed he did much better with one-on-one attention, but there was something more that drew her to him. There was a familiar spark in him that she couldn't quite explain, and they enjoyed each other's company tremendously.

"We could do twice as much today, huh?" he asked as he settled in across from her, his chair making a scraping sound as he scooted it closer to the table.

"Your homework done?" she asked, though it was really a rhetorical question. The papers he'd handed in so far had been well prepared, and his writing had become quite creative, filled with imaginative ideas and fantastical thoughts. She'd be willing to bet he'd jumped a grade level or more in his reading and comprehension even though he wouldn't be retested until he returned to his regular school in September.

In the month and a half they'd worked together, he'd blossomed. He'd started out so solemn and quiet, answering her questions with as few words as possible, and then only with what he thought she wanted to hear. Now that he was more confident, and she had earned his trust, she had learned to expect the unexpected from him.

"Can I ask you something?" she said as she reached for his papers. "I thought you didn't like school."

"Nah, I don't like the other kids sometimes. They make fun of me 'cause I don't pay attention all the time, and then I get in trouble 'cause I punch 'em. Besides, you make it fun—we just need more teachers like you."

She blushed at his heartfelt praise. "You, Hector, are a good student, and I don't want to find out you're in this program next year. You should spend next summer playing, having a good time."

He shrugged one shoulder. "I like it here at the college. Makes me feel . . . important."

"You *are* important. But you need to balance the serious stuff with the fun stuff, get involved with the other kids and have fun in the *real* world."

Hector's chin dropped to his chest. A sudden wave of déjà vu swept over Suzanne as she recognized her words to Hector were the same words that had come from her own sixth-grade teacher the day she'd been caught daydreaming in class one time too many.

Mr. Beecher had walked her to the office where she'd spent the rest of the afternoon talking with someone—the district psychologist, she'd found out later when her parents picked her up from school. Instead of going straight home, though, they'd stopped at Lake Murray for a family walk-and-talk, something they'd started when they had been her foster parents. Even after they'd adopted her, they continued the tradition. None of them said a word until they'd touched the gate that marked the three-mile point of return, and reversed their steps.

"What were you thinking about," her mother had asked, "that made your teacher so upset that she had me paged in the courtroom during my closing statement?"

Suzanne had felt bad about interrupting her parents' day. They worked hard at their jobs, and expected her to do the same in school. Many times they'd told her that *her* job *was* school. She'd been thinking about a favorite dream, reliving the sights and sounds of her desert dreamland, she remembered, but she didn't say so to her mother. "I already knew the lesson. It was boring and my mind just started to wander, I guess."

"But you need to pay attention. You have to try," her physics professor father had said.

"Darling, you're not really in trouble with us." Her mother had stopped, knelt in front of her, and gently held Suzanne's chin in her hand as she'd gazed into her eyes. "Maybe you could just find a way to . . . look more alert, that's all."

"Listen with one ear," her father had added.

"Okay," she'd replied. They'd spent the rest of the walk challenging each other to name the flowers using their Latin names, or identifying the occasional lizard that scampered across the pavement. Her father had even pulled from his pocket a piece of leftover bread he'd wrapped in a napkin, so she could feed the ducks. It had turned into a lovely family outing.

That day had been a turning point for her, and she'd decided then and there she'd never be in that kind of trouble again. She'd cringed when a couple of her classmates had sung the chorus of "Daydream Believer" as she'd been escorted out of the room that day. It had been humiliating, and she'd vowed the scene would never be repeated.

And it hadn't. She'd been a star student from that moment on, and she was certain the psychologist had added another success story to his professional portfolio.

Suzanne put her hand on the boy's. "Hector, let me start again," she said. He lifted his head to look at her, but his eyes were narrowed and she saw his jaw was clenched. "Please?" She waited until his face relaxed a little before she continued.

"Okay," he said softly.

"Why don't you take out your writing note-book—let's go outside. We'll talk while we walk, all right?"

He nodded and grabbed his dog-eared spiral notebook, and shoved a pencil in his shirt pocket. She led the way out of the quiet, stuffy library and into the commons, a square of green grass surrounded by buildings. Summer-semester students gathered in clumps, some sleeping, some chatting with their heads close to-gether. On a bench, a young man played guitar while two young women blissfully listened at his feet. On the farthest edge of the green she could see someone plucking a Celtic harp.

Much better. The sun was shining and the temperature was warm enough to want to seek out coveted patches of shade. She breathed deeply, drawing in the air as well as the image of the moment. Another one to remember.

"Where are we going?" Hector asked.

She'd almost forgotten he was beside her. "Over there." She pointed to where a cast iron bench sat under a fig tree. "That's my bench."

"What do you mean *your* bench?" he asked as he followed her, then sat down, opening his notebook to a clean page.

"Look," she said, and pointed to a small en-graved brass plaque on the back of the bench.

He read the lines out loud. "In memory of Pro-fessor Allister Lucas." He looked at her and smiled. "Hey—Lucas, that's your name."

She nodded. "Continue."

"Learn to be silent. Let your quiet mind listen and absorb. Py—py . . ." He stopped as he stumbled on the word.

"Py-thag-o-ras," she said, sounding out the syllables. "My father used to quote that all the time to me when I was little."

"What does it mean?"

"I want you to think about it for a while and when you're ready, write in your notebook what you think it means."

"Right now?"

"Yup."

"What are you going to do while I'm writing?"

She exhaled a deep breath. "Enjoy myself. Look at the scenery. If you take too long, I may take a nap—wake me up if I snore."

He giggled, then focused on the plaque as he nibbled on the end of his pencil. He stared at it a long time before he finally started scribbling his own words on the lined paper.

Suzanne could almost feel the vibration of the young boy's creativity as it was unleashed on the page. His spelling was atrocious, but he'd come up with some remarkable prose for a ten-year-old. She figured by the time he was using a computer, the spell-checker would become his best friend, so it didn't really matter. For now, she didn't grade on spelling, but only on creativity and originality; and once he'd realized that, he'd been getting nothing but As on his writing.

In the peaceful silence her eyelids began to feel

heavy, but she resisted the urge to close them, and instead concentrated on the wisps of white clouds in the brilliant blue sky. Hector liked to take his time, and she knew he'd be awhile. It was quiet in their little corner, except for the sound of him erasing and blowing away his changes.

She watched as the clouds moved in the wind and grew larger, a wisp at a time. The change of scenery had been a good idea. Her body relaxed until soon she felt completely at ease, every inch of her skin kissed by the summer breeze as it swooped down to the earth, then rose back up to the clouds again.

"It's you," she whispered, recognizing the gray-haired man sitting beside her on the bench. He was wearing the same blue and green plaid shirt and worn jeans, and he had the same smile she remembered. "Where's Hector?"

"This is a nice place," the man said. "There is much thinking that happens here."

"It's a good university," she agreed, "with fine teachers."

"Like your father. You miss seeing him here."

"Did you know him?"

"No, but I see him in your heart."

She blinked back sudden tears. She and her adoptive father had sat countless times on this bench together. It was true, but how could this man know? "I don't understand." The man patted her hand to comfort her. His felt callused and dry with age, but it also felt protective. His touch made her certain that he would be able to keep harm from coming too close to her; she felt utterly safe.

"Grieve no more for this man who chose to be your father, for it is only his physical journey that has ended. You were very precious to him, and he is proud of you."

She felt tears slip down her cheeks as she nodded at the old man.

"You and that man have the same burden: a strong mind that seeks answers by things that can be seen and touched. But there are many ways to see things, and many choices."

"Why did he have to die so young?"

"Only his flesh and physical mind are gone. This you know."

She nodded. Every time she sat on the bench, she felt a rush of warmth and love. Memories of her father whispered against her skin, along with the hot summer breeze.

"His spirit mind lives on, and he feels joy that you are beginning to listen to the inner voices, something he is just now learning to do."

"What voices?"

"He sees that you are seeking a balance, that you hear the voices of nature and spirit, that you might be willing to look beyond the prison of the flesh."

Suzanne's head began to spin. What was this

old man talking about? "Who *are* you?" she asked, focusing only on his eyes.

"You see me because I am able to live in both worlds," he explained.

*Two worlds? Impossible.* And the instant the thought solidified in her mind, the old man disappeared. When she blinked, it was Hector's face she stared at instead.

"Miss Lucas?" he whispered. "Are you okay?"

"Was I asleep?"

He shook his head, no. "But you sure had a funny look on your face—like you were daydreaming or something."

"You're sure I wasn't dozing?"

"Not unless you can sleep with your eyes open," he replied. "You want to hear what I wrote?"

She nodded, then looked away, returning her gaze to the sky.

"Okay," he began, "here goes."

As a cloud floated in front of the sun, goosebumps covered Suzanne's skin and she rubbed her arms.

Hector cleared his throat dramatically. "It's hard to be quiet when the world is running so fast that it trips over itself and falls to the ground, bruised and crying. Sometimes I can do it, though, if I try. If I find something to stare at, and listen only to the wind. If I can *become* the wind, then I can be silent and my mind gets quiet and I can really think. Not like I think all the time, but *really* think. Think like the eagle and the lizard and the butterfly. Think like the Earth Mother and the ocean and the tree. But I guess it's not really thinking after all; it's *being*."

He stopped, waiting for her reaction, and she looked at him. His brown eyes were filled with questions. "Perfect," she said, patting his hand. "You got it just right."

"Would your dad and Py ... Pythag ... o ... ras think so too?"

She felt a new wave of warmth as the sun emerged from the clouds again, and she lifted her face toward its rays. "Yup. They both would say it was exactly what the words meant."

Hector closed his notebook with a flourish, and he and Suzanne returned to the library to finish their lesson.

# Chapter Eighteen

She flopped onto her back and stared at the ceiling, wide awake. It had been a long time since she'd had a full night's sleep, and she'd finally connected the onset of the insomnia to when she and Hector had begun taking their writing lessons out to her father's bench.

Only able to catnap a few minutes at a time, she felt the accumulative negative effects of sleep deprivation. She'd hung up on Robin twice in the last week, snapped at Hector when he'd ask perfectly legitimate questions, and had almost fired the relocation company which she had contracted for the move. She was so sleepy during some days, she was even wondering about her ability to safely drive to Spring Lake.

She'd apologized to all and explained it was probably the stress of her move that made her impossible to be around. The worst part was the added sadness she felt because she so missed her dreamworld; she felt the insomnia was her punishment somehow. Totally illogical, she had concluded, but her emotions continued to zoom out of control anyway.

With a groan, she gave up, got out of bed and migrated to the couch, then flipped on the television. With any luck, an infomercial might lull her back to sleep.

She searched the channels for several moments, looking for a kitchen gadget demonstration to capture her attention, but she finally conceded and, instead, started packing books into boxes.

By the time the sun came up, the living room was completely packed. Each of the boxes was taped shut, labeled, and neatly stacked against the wall.

After a quick shower and a bowl of cereal, she had just enough time to mop the kitchen floor before she had to walk the half mile to the library for her final day with her students.

As she retrieved the mop and bucket, the phone rang.

"What are you doing?" Robin asked.

"Getting ready to mop the floor."

"Still having trouble sleeping?"

"Yeah. Got all the books packed, though."

"When are the movers coming?"

"They can't decide if it's going to be Monday or Tuesday," she said, cradling the phone on her shoulder as she leaned the mop against the counter. She could hear by the tone of Robin's voice that her friend was in a chatty mood; the floor would have to wait.

"So, no dreams to report?"

"Nothing I can remember, really. I keep having flashes during the day, though, which is weird. Just scenes and faces; nothing that makes any sense."

"It seems like things have flip-flopped, you know? Your *day*dreams are dominating, preventing you from—"

"Enough, Robin. I don't think I have the patience to talk about this right now. I'm too tired, and too emotional . . ."

"On a new subject," Robin continued, her voice still cheerful. "You get all your reports in on time?"

"Yup." Though her first two students' progress paled in comparison to Hector's, she had enjoyed seeing their self-esteem grow by leaps and bounds. She'd concluded they would most likely need continued individual academic help in the coming year. She had e-mailed her final notes to all her students' teachers, wrapping up the summer job.

"I e-mailed separately to Hector's teacher at the reservation school, and suggested she might consider finding him a mentor to encourage him with his creative writing. She already e-mailed back to say she had always suspected his literary talents, and promised it would be a priority to pair him up with someone who would continue to encourage his writing."

"You had a real impact on him, Suze."

"And he had a real impact on me. There's something about him, Robin, something really special. We connected, you know?"

"I know."

"Today's our last day."

"You sad?"

"It'll be a bittersweet time, I think. Good-byes are always hard, and this will be the start of many."

"Then promise me right now that we won't say them to each other," Robin said. "We'll just say see you soon and that's it."

"Okay, I promise."

"We're leaving tonight, Suze."

"What?!"

"Our moving truck guy called and offered us a great deal on a cancellation. We had to take it."

Suzanne looked up at the ceiling, fighting back tears. "I just won't let you go."

"You're leaving, too."

"But . . ." She could think of nothing to say. She and her best friend would be thousands of miles apart, beginning new lives that could take them anywhere.

"Suze?"

"I'm here."

"Think good thoughts for me, okay? I know you think I'm being impulsive and rash, but I really need to try this."

"I know, and I'm already thinking good thoughts for you."

"It might be a while before we get settled, so don't worry if you don't hear from me for a while, okay?" Robin's voice seemed shy and already distant.

"No, it's not okay. You e-mail me from an Internet cafe as soon as you set foot in Manhattan, or I'll never speak to you again." Robin's laughter rang in her ear, but was followed by a long silence.

"Okay, then," Robin finally said, her voice a little shaky. "You've got your last day of teaching to get through and I've got the rest of the packing."

"Right. See you soon, Robin."

"Seeya."

Suzanne hit the off button and closed her eyes. Only one hot tear escaped and made its way down her cheek while she waited for the ache in her heart to subside.

When she finally blinked open her eyes to check the clock, she had just enough time to get to the library before her first student.

"What do you mean it's closed?" Suzanne stood on the top of the marble stairs that led to the university library, face to face with a beefy security guard posted in front of the glass doors, blocking the main entrance.

"Exterminators are in there and no one is allowed in today. No one."

"But I have three students who are expecting—"

"I'll tell them the same thing I'm telling you."

"They're *children*, and it's our last day."

"I'll explain it to their parents."

"Fine!" She turned away and walked back down the stairs. Fine for the first two students, whose parents would be with them, but not for Hector. She'd just have to wait for him. Glancing at her watch, she figured she had about two hours until he'd be walking onto campus from the bus stop.

She positioned herself on the bottom step to consider her choices: she could go back home and pack a few things, or find something to do. Gazing at the commons in front of her, she watched as an older man and woman walked by, a freshly scrubbed freshman girl walking between them, obviously on a campus visit before the fall semester started. The young woman's eyes were wide and her head constantly turned as she looked in all directions, taking in the buildings and the ambience. Her face glowed with excitement.

Tilting her head, Suzanne carefully looked around at the campus, then exhaled a deep sigh. She'd miss the familiarity she felt here, and felt the twinge of homesickness already. *Stop it. The new campus will be just as fresh, just as enticing.* Logic said so, anyway. And she'd just have to find a way to cope. The flurry of class preparation and getting to know everyone would be her first distraction. She would be so busy, with any luck there would be little time to think . . . to remember. . . .

Rejecting the idea of packing up her office, she decided to take a memory walk around the college, her purpose to file away pictures in her mind: the Spanish architecture, how the new buildings mingled with the old, the carefully manicured patches of green, the lush palm trees and fuschia-colored thorny bougainvillea she loved so much.

First she retraced one of the many routes she'd used as a student; then she found herself walking toward the building where she taught—*used to teach*, she corrected herself. The door was open, and she walked in.

Breathing deeply, she wanted to remember every sight and smell of the place where she'd lectured in front of her first roomful of eager students. She walked up to the room, but it was being cleaned, so she walked on. *Good—out with the old and in with the new.*

With another half hour to kill, she strolled back toward the commons, and finally to the bench under the fig tree. It would be a long time before she'd be able to come back for a visit, and the luxury of time alone in her favorite spot was an unanticipated treat.

Her fingers touched the brass plaque, then rested on her father's name as she traced the letters. Her mother had immediately loved the idea of the bench when Suzanne had suggested it shortly after her father's unexpected death. The faculty and his students had collected money for a donation to S.A.D.D., but they'd also wanted to do something on campus in his honor. Her father had brought students to the site under the fig tree for his lecture series on Richard Feynman's unconventional view of physics. It was one of his favorite courses, and he'd insisted that Mr. Feynman would have approved. In tribute to the legendary scientist, he'd begun each lecture with a short improvisational piece played on the bongo drums. It made his students fall in love with him every time.

After a glance at her watch, Suzanne rose from the bench and made her way back to the library. When she saw Hector at the top of the steps talking to the security guard, she ran the rest of the way. The guard was standing with his arms crossed, shaking his head, and she could see Hector refusing to budge.

"Hector!" she called. "I'm here!"

He turned and ran down the steps, concern pinching his face. "I didn't know what to do—"

"I know, I know. Bummer, huh? It's our last day, and we can't even *have* a last day."

He looked at her, both eyebrows raised. "There isn't a bus home until four."

"How about you come with me to my apartment and we'll call your mom?"

He nodded, then grinned. "We'll have a last day anyway?"

"You betcha."

They walked silently to Suzanne's apartment, and Hector followed her into the kitchen so he could call his mother.

"*Háawka 'ememaa.*"

Suzanne's ears pricked at his words and a shiver zoomed up her spine that caused her scalp to tickle. She knew what he had said. *Hello, mommy.* She stared at Hector, her lips slightly parted in wonder.

"I'm fine," he said into the phone, "but the library is closed today—I'm at Miss Lucas's house." He listened intently and then put his hand over the mouthpiece and turned toward her. "My mom said she could get a ride here with someone who's coming into San Diego today. And then we could take a different bus home together if you give her the address."

"That sound good to you?"

He nodded and handed her the phone.

While she gave Hector's mother her address, Suzanne watched Hector scrutinize the room, his gaze jumping from half-filled boxes to empty cupboards with their doors wide open, to a variety of take-out containers that littered the counter. When the call ended, she walked to the refrigerator.

"You want some lemonade?" she asked.

"Sure. Why's all your stuff in boxes?"

She grabbed two glasses off the dish drainer and poured their drinks. "Well, I'm finishing up packing to move."

"Where?"

"I have a new teaching job at a university in the northern part of California. The University of Spring Lake—sounds nice, huh?"

"Sure," he said as he took a seat at the kitchen table, unloaded his backpack and placed his notebooks to one side.

She put one glass in front of him and joined him at the table.

"Don't you like it here?" he asked.

She stared at him as he gulped down half the lemonade in two long swallows. "I love it here, but it's a great opportunity for me. I'll have the chance to start up their first department of ethnobotany—that's what I do when I'm not doing what I do with you," she explained.

"So you'll be the boss?"

"Yup. Kinda cool, huh?"

He nodded. "But you don't seem that happy about it."

She took a few swallows from her own glass before she dared answer—even Hector could see through what she had thought of as a perfectly constructed facade. "Well," she began, "I am very excited about being the department head, but I wish the university was closer to here. This is where I grew up, and I'm going to miss it very much."

His brows furrowed as he absorbed her explanation. "Is your family here?"

"Well, no. You know my dad died, and after that, my mom moved back East to be closer to her brother and sister."

"Oh. It sort of sounded to me like you would be missing your people," he said quietly.

As the words left the boy's lips, Coyote's face materialized in her mind, and in an instant she knew exactly how she would feel when she left.

She would miss the desert, but it was more than that. Her greatest fear was that her dreamworld would be left behind, as well. The desert, her dreamworld, and Coyote.

"Are you okay, Miss Lucas?"

She blinked. How long had she been sitting there with her glass in the air, halfway to her lips, frozen in time? "I'm fine, Hector. I was just thinking about stuff I'm going to miss, that's all. And that includes you, too."

He grinned. "You'll always be my favorite teacher, forever. I don't care how many teachers I have the rest of my life."

She returned his smile. "Let's get started, okay?" She reached for his notebook to read his final assignment.

The sound of their shared raucous laughter almost drowned out the soft tap on the front door. When she finally heard it, Suzanne welcomed Hector's mother, then led the woman through the living room and to the kitchen where her son was gathering his things.

"*Háawka*, Hector," the boy's mother said in a low, composed voice.

Hector's face lit up when he saw her, and he

finished stuffing his backpack and zipped it up. "This is Miss Lucas, Mom."

Suzanne extended her hand to the woman, who grasped it firmly. "It's a pleasure to meet you, and I have to confess your son has been my favorite student."

The woman offered a small, shy smile, then said, "He speaks about you so much at home—I'm glad we had this chance to meet." Then she reached into her pocket. "I brought you a gift, to thank you for the encouragement you've given my son. I'm sure he will have a much better year this year, because of you."

Suzanne looked down at an intricately woven miniature basket that the woman cradled in her hand, then took it from her. Inside the basket, a piece of carved rose quartz hung from a knotted leather cord.

"How beautiful," she whispered as she picked up the stone to examine it more carefully. It was a coyote, sitting on its haunches with its nose pointed skyward, mouth open in a howl.

"I know you will think this is strange," she said, "but I had a dream that you should have this necklace. And I made the basket myself—something I learned when I was a girl."

Suzanne stared into the woman's dark eyes. *A coyote?* She was speechless, unable to force words from her brain to her mouth. She slipped the necklace over her head. "It's perfect," she said, fingering the smooth stone. "Do you have

time to sit for a moment; to have something cold
to drink before you go?"

"Yes, thank you. Our bus won't come for
about thirty minutes."

Suzanne poured another glass of lemonade
and refilled the two glasses already on the table.
She and Hector's mother chatted several minutes
about the progress he'd made, and his talent for
writing. For the first time, his mother explained,
he was looking forward to the beginning of the
school year. Hector remained silent, suddenly
shy now that his mother was there.

After she'd finished her lemonade, Hector's
mother asked, "May I tell you something, Miss
Lucas?"

"Certainly," Suzanne said. She met the
woman's gaze.

"When I look in your eyes, I think you have
not been sleeping well at night for some time.
Am I right?"

Suzanne drew her eyebrows together into a
frown. *Was it that obvious?* "I've had insomnia
about a month now. I've tried everything, but
nothing seems to help."

"There is an old woman at the reservation; she
lives next door to us and she knows the old
ways. She might be able to help you if you could
come visit for the weekend."

Suzanne suddenly felt very uncomfortable.
"Oh, I don't know. The movers are maybe coming on Monday, and I have to finish packing
and—"

"I see in your eyes that you are weary, weary to your bones. And in my dream there was a message for me to tell all this to you. Ah, perhaps it's just silly words from a silly dream. No matter." The woman patted her hand, then gestured to Hector to get ready.

Suzanne stood, then pulled the boy to her in a quick hug, releasing him before he had a chance to squirm free. "You have important things to say, Hector, and I want you to keep writing, okay?"

"I promise," he mumbled as he looked down at his feet.

She watched as he and his mother walked through the apartment and out the front door. Hand in hand, they went down the sidewalk and around the corner, and finally out of sight.

Suzanne closed the door, then leaned her back against it and thought about the woman's words. It was so strange, so illogical. She fingered the smooth surface of the pendant and closed her eyes. Her entire body was exhausted; she felt so, so tired. She knew if she could just get a couple nights of good sleep, everything would be all right.

*I should go with them.* The thought reverberated in her brain, completely out of control with its intensity. Then, without another second's hesitation, she ran into her bedroom and stuffed a change of clothes into her daypack, added her cosmetic bag, and finally her wallet. She grabbed her keys off the kitchen counter, and locked the door behind her. If she hurried, she could pick Hector and his mother up at the bus stop and give them both a ride home.

Whether her dreamworld was impossibly silly or not, she could at least see what the old woman had to say.

# Chapter Nineteen

Suzanne followed Hector and his mother into their modest home on the Barona reservation. It was immaculate, and tastefully decorated with an eclectic mix of modern and ancient artwork. She felt completely at ease and welcome in the tiny house.

"Sit, sit," Hector's mother said as she pulled out a high-backed oak chair.

Suzanne dropped into it, still amazed to be sitting in the woman's kitchen instead of her own, packing. Hector had been delighted, his initial embarrassment unable to compete with his expressed feeling of excitement about his plans to show off his teacher to the rest of his family and friends.

"We'll have something to eat now, because you might not have a chance later," his mother explained.

"Just what can I expect?" Suzanne asked.

"Delfina is very old, blind, and she doesn't

speak English, only an old dialect of *Kumeyaay*. She will figure out what to do to help you. Hector might be able to interpret some; he studies our language in school and is more fluent than I am," she added, pride coloring her voice.

Suzanne ate, while Hector chatted eagerly about the places he planned to show her the next day if she stayed over, and he said that she could spend the night in the guest room next to his room.

After dinner, he, Suzanne and his mother walked several yards to the one-room adobe house where the old woman lived. Suzanne's stomach tightened as she walked, but instantly relaxed when she crossed the threshold to step into the little house. The wooden plank door closed behind them, the room darkened dramatically and she stood still as her eyes adjusted to the dimness.

An oil lamp on the floor in one corner was the only source of light, and as her eyes grew more accustomed to the darkness, she felt Hector's hand in her own as he led her toward the lamp. Next to it, sitting on a blanket, was a very elderly woman. Every inch of her face was creased with deep lines and wrinkles, and Suzanne thought the woman looked at least a century old. She looked into the woman's sightless black eyes, surprised how they twinkled with life.

"*Háawka, 'Aashaa nemeshap.*" The woman's face collapsed into a smile, and she pointed to the blanket-covered straw directly in front of her.

"What'd she say, Hector?" Suzanne asked. He seemed baffled for a moment, then shrugged one shoulder before he answered her.

"I'm not sure why, but she called you White Bird."

Suzanne's mind reeled first with confusion, then with inexplicable recognition. She had the strange thought that the woman was precisely accurate in calling her that; and for whatever reason, it felt exactly right. *'Aashaa nemeshap.* She *was* White Bird.

As her knees began to quiver, she was glad to sit down, and she tugged Hector's hand to let him know she wanted him to sit beside her. His mother remained standing behind them.

The old woman faced Suzanne, their knees almost touching, and her dark eyes stared blankly in the direction of Suzanne's chest. Finally the old woman brought a gnarled hand out of her lap and reached it forward.

Suzanne forced herself not to flinch as the crone leaned forward, then leaned closer and closer until her face was finally within a foot of her own. Keeping her eyes focused on the old woman's black eyes, Suzanne watched her shift her blind gaze upward toward her hair.

With one hand, the old woman patted the curls at the side of Suzanne's head and laughed softly. Then she brought her hand in front again and lifted Suzanne's bangs with her fingers and traced the wavy tattooed line with the thumb of her other hand. Joy bubbled in her crackly laugh, and her smile seemed to broaden in approval. Then she said a few words.

"Hector, what's going on?" Suzanne whispered, forcing her lips into a tight smile. "How can she know about the mark on my forehead? And why does she seem so pleased?"

"The only word I understood was *wekwiich*. It means tattoo," he said, then leaned forward and tipped his head back to look at her. "Where'd you get it?"

"I don't know," Suzanne admitted, halfheartedly hoping the old woman might be able to provide the answer.

Both she and Hector listened as the old woman chattered away. Finally Hector began to speak. "She says that you were very sick, and the mark was put on you during a special ceremony."

Suzanne reached up and touched her forehead with her fingertips. It had been . . . a *healing* ceremony. *Why do I know that?*

Hector continued. "She says she has something your body needs, something that will help you sleep."

The woman reached to the side, then carefully poured liquid into a cup and held it out toward Suzanne.

"What's that?" she asked.

"She says that if you will drink it, no harm will come to you. It will put you to sleep almost right away, and you'll wake up like you've been reborn. You'll feel really good, and you'll be rested. She says it will be good for you."

"You think it's safe?"

Hector nodded. "I got some herbs and stuff from her lots of times when I was sick. It always worked. Usually it tastes really bad, but I always got better fast."

The woman held the cup closer to Suzanne, and spoke again.

Hector translated. "She's saying something about your dreams. Something about how you'll be able to remember them all, after you sleep. Does that make sense?"

This time, it was Suzanne who nodded. "Yes. Okay, I guess I'm ready." She took the cup from the woman, who immediately seemed overjoyed at her decision. She sniffed the liquid. The aroma seemed slightly bitter, but it also had a fruity smell.

"You might want to hold your nose and chug it," Hector suggested.

She gave him a nervous grin, then pinched her nostrils and drank the liquid in several successive swallows.

"Was it awful?" he asked.

"Not too bad, really," she said. She leaned forward and returned the cup to the woman's outstretched hands. When she leaned back, a wave of dizziness swirled through her head and she put both palms on the ground to steady herself.

"We should get you back to the guest room," Hector's mother said.

Suzanne felt a surge of euphoria as she pushed

herself to her feet, and she allowed Hector and his mother to help her out the door. The desire to lie down and sleep was strong. It was all she could do to stay awake for the walk back to Hector's house and the bed that awaited her there.

Suzanne's eyes fluttered, finally opening to peer into the dimly lit room. She pulled her arms out from beneath the light blanket that covered her up to her chin.

"You awake?" Hector whispered.

"How long have I been asleep?" Her throat was so parched, she had difficulty getting the words to come out. She rubbed her eyes, then took the glass of water he offered. The cool liquid helped to rouse her a little more, and soothed the dryness in her mouth and throat.

"You want some more? The old woman said you would be really thirsty when you woke up."

She drank another glass and handed it back to him, then sat up in the small bed and looked around. "It's dark."

"You slept all night and all day. You feel better?"

As the fog in her mind began to clear, she realized how good she did feel. She nodded, then stretched her arms. "I feel like a new person, like I slept a hundred years."

"Don't worry," he said, "it's just tomorrow. Nothing's changed."

But things *had* changed. She closed her eyes for a moment to isolate exactly what was different. The instant her eyelids rested, a rush of pictures raced through her mind. She blinked open her eyes and the images vanished. When she closed them again, the pictures resumed, this time like a fast-forwarded video. There was no sound, but details were crystal clear.

Dream images from her childhood came first—the Indian boy as he grew up, and sometimes the gray-haired man was there with him. Then a blank screen, and slowly Coyote's face materialized. Building a fire. Swimming with him in the pond. Him nursing her wounds. The sandals he made for her. The miners and the shack. The sandstorm. Then another blank screen.

She gasped and opened her eyes. Hector had moved closer to the bed, and she stared into his wide eyes and serious face. "I remember," she whispered.

"She said to bring you to her when you woke up."

"Let's go." She pushed aside the blanket and followed him. The memories of her dreams were clear, but her memories of Coyote were lucid—as though she had lived them and not simply dreamed them. She pushed aside all logic and entered the old woman's house, ready for answers to the dozens of questions that filled her mind.

She had awakened feeling like a new person, but she had a strange sense that she had actually *become* a new person.

Hector held open the door for her, and Suzanne entered the dimly lit room. Again, the oil lamp sat in the corner and provided a yellow pool of light next to the old woman. Again, a gnarled finger pointed to the blanket.

Suzanne sat down, and Hector sat beside her but closer this time to the old woman. She spoke softly, then extended one hand to the boy. He grasped it, then grasped Suzanne's fingers with his other hand.

"She says it will help me translate." He shrugged one shoulder. "Couldn't hurt, right?"

Suzanne nodded and hoped the three-way link would provide some additional emotional strength. She felt she was going to need it; the fear factor had increased ten-fold.

The old woman spoke for a few minutes while Hector listened intently, occasionally cocking his head and furrowing his brow. Finally he nodded and turned to Suzanne.

"She says while you were sleeping she visited your dreams. That's why you didn't dream this time. She met a man called Coyote, and also his grandfather who is a *kuseyaay*—it's like a shaman—to his people. He's teaching Coyote to be one now. She said to tell you it was the gray-haired man, and that you would know who she meant. Then she said the man called Coyote told her a story about White Bird—I'm guessing that's you, right?"

Suzanne nodded, her mind growing numb.

Hector stopped and listened to the old woman

again for a few minutes, then cleared his throat and continued. "Coyote is happy you are here, because he is waiting for you near the *Senyaweche* village. He has waited a long time. He said to tell you the old woman can help you, *if* you want to come back. He said it is your choice."

He was waiting for her. Was it really possible? Could she actually find a way to go back? It was a crazy thought, but it burned inside her anyway. She closed her eyes and Coyote's face materialized, a tiny smile curving his lips. Barely aware of the dialogue that continued between Hector and the old woman, she listened instead to the quickening thud of her heart.

"Miss Lucas?"

She felt Hector's hand tugging on hers, and she reluctantly opened her eyes. "How could I go back?"

"She says you are special, because . . . most people don't understand about the two worlds—I think that's what she meant. She says you have the gift. Your dreams have always been real, and she says you knew that, even when you were a little girl. Your *temeshaa*—your spirit—has been able to enter this other place. I'm not sure I got that part right—"

"What part?"

"Well, I think she said you are special like the shamans. And because you wanted to be in this other place so much, in your dreams you were able to actually go there. But you always came back here, to this world. Then she said during the earthquake, a window or something like that opened."

"Like a portal?"

"Yeah! And so your *awake-self* actually went there."

"I don't understand—it seemed like I was gone a long time, but while I was gone, time didn't go by here at all."

"She talked about time, a little, and how time doesn't act the same in the two places. She said shamans can go forward and back in their own world, and how they can cross over into this other world and go forward and backward, too. It's kinda confusing."

*No kidding.* "So, when I'm dreaming, I actually exist in this other place?"

"I think so, at least temporarily."

"But I exist here, too?"

"I know this sounds dumb, but the way she was talking it sounded kind of like you have a stunt double." He grinned, waiting for her response.

"A stunt double. Like an alternate me? Hector, this sounds pretty crazy—you know that, don't you?"

"I think it's cool. I'm gonna start writing down my dreams and see if it's more interesting there than here."

"Okay, if it's possible to have me here *and* there, why did I come back?"

"She said that there was another storm or

something. Sometimes the earth's energy gets weird—like in an earthquake—and the window opened up again."

"So I came back even if I didn't want to?"

He shrugged. "I guess you couldn't control it. I think now that you know, and if you accept, you get to choose—"

"She really said I could go back?"

"I think what she's saying is that you can become your dream-self if you really want to, and that other self will be here . . . just like normal."

Suzanne brought the fingers of her free hand to the bridge of her nose and tried to pinch away the headache that had formed. It was too much to absorb. *Parallel lives?* And that somehow she had crossed into some other plane, on another timeline—but she could somehow live in both worlds? It was more than impossible; it was nuts.

Suzanne's thoughts were interrupted by the touch of the old woman's hand on her knee. She listened while the woman spoke softly, watched her expression grow more serious.

After a few moments, Hector translated. "She says you get to choose: you can only see Coyote in your dreams, or you can make the switch and let your conscious spirit go there to be with him. Your other self will continue to live here. No one will know the difference . . . except you, of course."

"I need some time to think this through."

Hector nodded. "She told me to take you back

to my house so you can rest and think, and then you can come back to see her if you want to know how to make the journey."

She watched as the old woman dropped Hector's hand, and he jumped to his feet to help her up.

"You can use the shower in the hallway just outside your room," he said as he guided her through the yard and back toward the house. "Mom's cooking, and we can have supper together, okay?"

"Sounds great, Hector. And thank-you for your translation, by the way. Pretty impressive." He grinned in response, and she was pretty sure he was blushing. Inside, he walked toward the kitchen to help with the meal preparation while she continued on to her room. There she grabbed her daypack. After a hot shower, she knew it would be easier to think and decide what she was going to do.

# Chapter Twenty

Suzanne wiped the condensation from the mirror and then combed her hair away from her face. She stared at her reflection and lifted a finger to trace the tattoo, just as the old woman had done.

She would go back . . . to him. Crazy or not.

The decision made, her reflection smiled back as she dried her hair with a towel and quickly slipped into clean clothes. Her stomach rumbled loudly as she brushed her teeth then repacked her bag.

After supper, Hector tipped his head and grinned. "Well?"

Matching his grin with her own, she nodded and followed him back to the old woman's house. Without hesitation, she walked in and sat in front of her.

Hector joined her, and the woman began speaking rapidly.

Suzanne felt like she was in a movie where the

ending was just about to happen but she had absolutely no idea how things were going to turn out. Her scalp tingled and goosebumps formed on her arms.

The old woman reached into the darkness to a spot next to her hip, then brought out a lidded gourd and a folded piece of leather. Hector took the items and placed them on the blanket.

"What's that?" Suzanne asked.

"Something more to drink, but not now," he explained. "She keeps saying you're supposed to go to the place where the new water flows. The only thing I can think of that she might mean is where the Old Mission Dam is, in Mission Trails park. We went on a field trip there once, and the ranger talked about how our people built the dam and the aqueduct."

"Maybe." It sounded convincing. The dam had certainly brought new water to the mission ... but how long ago? A couple hundred years, at least.

"Anyway," he continued, "you're supposed to go there, drink what's in here, and put the deer-skin on."

"And when is this supposed to happen?"

"This is the part I don't get. She says you have to go there when the stars fall from the sky."

Suzanne looked from Hector to the woman and back again.

"*Hellytaa.*" The old woman laughed, then reached toward Suzanne and patted her curls, then touched her own hair.

"What's she saying about my hair, Hector?"

"Did you used to have long hair?" he asked.

"Yes, but . . . I cut it all off one night."

"She says to tell you it is the way of a *Kumeyaay* woman—it is an act of mourning. When you dreamed that first night, you were caught between the two worlds. You cut your hair because you mourned your return to *this* world, and for losing the man called Coyote."

Tears filled her eyes, along with the relief she felt to know why she had done it. Why she had done everything. *The way of a Kumeyaay woman.*

There was a life she'd been wanting, repressing, needing. It explained her hesitation in the past. And now, was she about to be fulfilled?

"Hector, will you ask her something for me?"

"Sure, if I can."

"Ask her how she knows."

Before Hector had time to translate, the old woman reached for Suzanne's hands and held them tightly in her own. " '*Ehemach 'ewuuws, 'Aashaa nemeshap.*"

"Hector?"

"She said she saw it in her dreams, Miss Lucas."

The woman yawned, and Hector tipped his head toward the door. Suzanne picked up the deerskin and the gourd and they left. Neither one spoke as they walked. She paused at her car and put the two items on the passenger seat, then followed him into the house.

"I should get my daypack," she said. He followed her to the guestroom and stood in the doorway, shifting his weight from one foot to the other. "Hector, are you going to tell your mother about all this?"

"Nope. The old woman said it was for your ears only. She also said I'd forget any of this ever happened by morning."

"Oh, Hector . . ."

"I don't want to forget. This is the coolest thing that's ever happened to me."

"Then go right now and write everything down, just in case. Who knows, you might put it in a book someday."

"You really think I can be a writer?"

"Hector, you already are. You just have to keep writing. Write every day—write about everything that happens in your life and in other people's lives. Your world will grow larger because of it, I promise you that."

His face glowed, and he looked directly back at her. "I promise I'll keep writing. And I'll do better in school this year, I know it."

She slipped one of the pack's straps over her shoulder, then pulled him to her for a long hug and finally released him. "I'll miss you. No matter what happens—"

"Hey, I might see you in *my* dreams. You never know."

She smiled. "You never know. Will you tell your mother thank-you for me? I think I really have to go."

"Sure."

As she drove down the road, she glanced in the rear-view mirror at the glowing windows of Hector's house, and then at the dark shape of the old woman's house next door, the windows just a lighter shade of dark. It all seemed even more unreal now that she was behind the wheel and leaving the experience behind.

She shivered and rolled up her window, then flipped on the radio to distract her thoughts for a while, at least until she got home. There, perhaps, she could sort out what had happened and what, realistically, her next step would be. Or, maybe she would come to her senses.

She pressed the radio buttons until she found a newscast.

*. . . and you'll find the temperatures tomorrow will be pretty much a carbon copy of today's, with the usual night and morning low clouds that should burn off by noon at the beaches, much earlier in the inland areas. And now, a special report on an astronomical delight. . . .*

*Just before mid-August is the time to stay up late— find a spot away from the streetlights and porchlights and look up. Tonight is the night for the best viewing of the Perseids, and though these meteors typically are only the size of an apple seed, they travel thirty-seven miles per second. But don't worry about one falling from the sky and ruining your star party . . . each one is somewhere between fifty and one hundred and twenty miles away.*

*One guarantee: that magical streak across the sky will elicit a healthy gasp every time. Best viewing?*

Janet Wellington

*From a reclining position with as big an expanse of clear sky above you as you can find. Zenithal activity—the number of meteors you see per hour—this year promises to be between fifty and one hundred, depending on the absence of haze and clouds in our southern California skies, and how far from the city lights you are. Peak time is between midnight and four A.M. So, good luck with your star gazing. Now, back to late-night jazz . . .*

Stars falling from the sky.

"This is crazy," Suzanne muttered as she turned off the radio. *Tonight*? She glanced at the deerskin and gourd on the seat beside her and groaned. There was no time to contemplate all her options, weigh the pros and cons, or do any of her usual reflection before making a major decision. She had to let her heart make the decision this time. But could she?

# *Chapter Twenty-one*

She pulled her Honda into a parking space near the Visitor and Interpretive Center of Mission Trails Regional Park.

*Where the new water flows.* "I hope you're right, Hector." The river had been there forever, but the flume built by the Indians for the mission had been how the water had been brought to the whites.

The new water.

She'd been to the park dozens of times with her students to identify the plants of a riparian habitat. The streamside thickets along the San Diego River offered the perfect backdrop, easily accessible examples of sycamore, cottonwood, and willow for the basic native plant lecture she preferred to give in the field.

She turned off the ignition and looked around. The parking lot was empty except for what appeared to be a ranger's vehicle. It was late, and she wouldn't likely meet anyone along the Father Junipero Serra Trail that would lead her to the historic Old Mission Dam. It would be an easy walk on the paved two-lane road that made up most of the trail. The moonglow would be adequate to navigate the less than two-mile walk, so she left her flashlight in the glove box.

Pulling her things from her daypack, she put the deerskin and the gourd inside, then slipped her arms through the straps as she got out of her seat. She shoved her keys in her pocket, then pulled them out again and stared at them in the palm of her hand.

She knelt with one knee on the pavement and placed them out of sight on the top of the front tire, which was her habit if she had nowhere else to stash them.

Before she could change her mind, she turned away and began to walk. After a few moments she slowed her pace, hoping her thumping heart might do the same. *This is crazy*. The thought played like a mantra in her head, keeping time with her steady steps.

The air was warm and saturated with the aromas of the plants that grew along the side of the road. Healthy bushes of black sage stood almost six feet tall, and the minty fragrance dominated the scents she inhaled as she walked. Along the right side of the road, the towering cliffs and hills threw black shadows onto her path.

For centuries, the *Kumeyaay* had coexisted in the area with nature and all that was provided. The environment afforded everything they'd needed: tule reeds and juncas for thatching and baskets, quartz for arrow tips, clay for pottery, plentiful food. A garden of Eden, she thought. No—Shangri-La, but quite real.

As she walked, she remembered more and more of her desert dreamworld. She no longer had to close her eyes to see and recall the images from that lifetime of dreams. And the time spent with Coyote was clearly a memory, her mind now easily able to distinguish between remembrance and imagination and dream.

She no longer doubted that what the old woman told Hector must be true. Otherwise, how could she have the deep feelings she had? She loved Coyote. And she wanted more than anything to be with him. If her dream-self and she could trade places, why not? Her brain debated the same question over and over as she walked until finally she stopped in her tracks and shouted to the sky, "Enough!"

She kept her gaze upward as she made a slow circle where she stood, taking in the sparkle of the stars, the sound of the slight breeze as it rustled the bushes and trees around her, and the subtle waves of warmth that rose from the asphalt below her feet.

For several minutes she stood, forcing herself to quiet her mind and think of nothing. Nothing but Coyote's face and how her heart ached to return to him.

Finally, she looked down at the road and put one foot in front of the other, focusing only on the pavement before her. And she kept walking.

When she found herself in the small, deserted parking lot at the dam end of the park, she hurried past the educational signs to make her way to the part of the structure that had been preserved as an historic look at what many referred to as an uncomfortable past—a past filled with forced labor of the indigenous people of the area and, eventually, a forcing of the people to leave their Shangri-La to make room for ranchers and farmers who bought the land from other whites who claimed it.

She understood Coyote's anger, and she would be able to help him if she remembered modern times upon her return to her dreamworld.

After crossing the narrow expanse of the river, she found an open area and emptied her daypack, placing the deerskin and gourd on a flat rock. Then she undressed and wrapped herself in the soft deerskin. It felt good against her skin . . . familiar. She ran her palm against the lovely smoothness of the surface.

She sat on the ground and leaned back against the boulder so she was almost lying down. The expanse of clear sky above her was large, and would provide an ideal viewing space for the meteor shower to come.

As she stared at it, the night sky almost seemed to be shimmering, but even after she rubbed her eyes, the sky still flickered. Time, too, felt strange. Hours or minutes passed, she wasn't sure, when finally the first streak across the sky caused her to gasp in surprise and delight.

"Beautiful," she whispered.

Another and another streak followed, and she reached for the gourd then sat up. Could she do this? Give up everything to go back? Did she think this was craziness? No. And she loved Coyote that much. She drank the liquid.

It was sweet, and it also had a slight fizziness that tickled her throat as she swallowed. She licked a droplet from her lips and smiled, then reclined again. Any lingering doubts vanished as she felt a surge of velvet warmth spread from the pit of her stomach until all of her tingled. Her fingertips and her toes prickled with a strange sensation, and even her earlobes felt like they were being pricked by pins and needles.

The stars looked closer, somehow, and she reached up thinking she could actually touch them—and she was delighted to suddenly be able to feel the sky. *It feels like jelly, but thinner and stickier*, she thought. And when she brought her fingers back, they glittered with starlight. The sparkle traveled up her arms and filled her with a delicious feeling of effervescence.

*I am the stars and the sky.*

It was her last thought before her eyes grew heavy and she fell into a deep sleep. In her dreams she leapt from star to star in a crazy dance. In the night sky she twirled and spun; then she jumped on the tail of a falling star, riding it until it faded away to nothingness.

\* \* \*

Suzanne stirred. Her body felt like it weighed four hundred pounds in comparison to the lightness of her dream-self that had danced with the celestial bodies. She hesitated to open her eyes, afraid she would return to the reality she'd decided to wish with all her heart to leave behind.

Softness tickled her leg as a small creature leaned against her. *A kitten?* she wondered. Unable to resist her curiosity, she opened her eyes a tiny crack—just enough to focus on the living thing lying so still beside her. A coyote pup cuddled closer against her leg, and she smiled as her eyes closed again and sleep instantly returned.

This time, she floated and flew through the night air just above the trees, following the flight of an owl as it soared through the sky. At last, she sensed she should halt and drop to the land. She spotted a clearing and floated down to the grass where a man was waiting for her.

" '*Aashaa nemeshap*, my heart sings."

"Are you real?"

Coyote opened his arms, and Suzanne eagerly stepped into them. As his arms encircled her, she buried her hands in his hair and snuggled against the corded muscles of his chest. The touch of his smooth hot skin against hers made her tremble with immediate desire.

Lifting her head, she breathed a kiss against his neck and he moaned, then pulled her tighter against him. Wriggling in his grasp, she stood

284

on tiptoe and moved her lips to touch his mouth.
His lips pressed hard against hers, and then
gently covered her mouth as he returned the kiss
with a hunger that sent waves of pleasure
through her.

When they finally parted, she was breathless.
He moved his lips and showered kisses around
her mouth and along her jaw, then dropped to
her shoulders and her neck. She felt her knees
weaken as his head descended to her breasts. His
hair slid like silk against her arm as she pulled
him down, leading his mouth to one breast and
holding him there her until the passion he created spread lower and lower, until she thought
she could stand it no more.

Gently he pulled away and eased her to the
ground. He knelt beside her and a smile spread
across his face that ended in his eyes. His hand
caressed each swollen nipple until she felt a
shudder building between her legs; then she felt
his hand slide intimately across her belly and to
her thigh. She pushed herself against his touch,
and his hands continued searching, rubbing,
moving gently along her body until every inch
of her skin tingled and she quivered with longing.

The moan she heard was her own, a deep, tormented, animal sound that made his eyes grow
darker; he hadn't stopped looking at her while
his hands explored her body. She reached for his
shoulders and pulled him to her, then closer so

she could slide under him. Her body was half ice and half flame as she felt his chest heavy against her breasts.

For a moment they simply held each other, then he moved and gently entered her. In an instant, her body seemed like liquid fire and she arched against him. They moved together, and she surrendered to the searing need she was sure had been building within her all her life. Finally, it would be fulfilled. And on her terms.

Her breath came in long moans, and her senses spun with emotions fed by the flames within her. She felt the passion in Coyote grow, and he lifted his head and looked into her eyes. Gladly she followed him to ecstasy, falling into the perfect sensation of their bodies moving together. Passion arced like lightning between them, through them. A tremor inside her radiated from the soft core of her body, and she abandoned herself to the hot tide as it swelled and raged and finally peaked as she cried out loud and a million stars exploded around her.

Waves of passion continued to throb through her as she felt him climb his own peak, then tense, then release. He searched for her lips to reclaim them with his own, and his mouth covered hers hungrily. He kissed her until his body relaxed. Moving her hands to his face, she pulled his head away to nestle against her neck and waited until his tortured breathing began to calm.

Her hands caressed the planes of his back and

he settled, finally, against her, his body completely at rest. Flesh against flesh they were naked in each other's arms; skin to skin they were as one.

Suzanne knew the sun was just coming up, the first light of the new day was dancing along her cheek. The sensation filled her with wonder, and she'd never felt so in tune with herself and her surroundings.

The air was sweet and the day promised to be warm and mild. The summer would soon end. The thought didn't bother her, but instead added to her sense of wonder. She felt as though her future was a clean slate. Nothing was determined, nothing predestined.

Each day was a new future, a chance to change or grow or stay the same. It didn't matter.

She sighed and focused on the movement of the sun, now warming her chin. She stayed still until her face felt kissed by the rays, the day's gentle heat a hint of what might come. But was she where she wanted to be? Where had she awoke?

A shadow blocked the sun. *A cloud?* She furrowed her brow, then opened her eyes to focus on the face of Coyote.

" *'Aashaa nemeshap*—are you real?" he whispered.

Suzanne nodded, then threw herself into his arms. "My heart sings!" She was real, he was real, and they no longer needed to live through their dreams.

# Epilogue
## for Two Lives

*Suzanne Lucas.* When I remember how I struggled with the decision to move north, I find the details have blurred over the years. Logic reminds me that of course it's difficult to leave familiar people and places behind, but it always seems like there was more to it than that.

No matter . . . my perfect job at the university is even better than I'd imagined—the dazzle, for once, was real. The one thing that remains crystal clear to me was hearing Robin's voice in my head the minute I set foot on the property, reminding me, "Life's supposed to be about taking chances." She'd found paradise in New York and she was delighted I'd found mine where I least expected.

And it wasn't long before I was certain I was in the right place at the right time. I remember feeling it as I walked onto the campus the first day, and this is the thought that remains so strong, these many years later.

I met my husband because I moved here. He interviewed me for the local paper and proceeded to steer my life onto an unexpected path, as love will do sometimes. Besides writing, his passion is the sea, and I began to research the potential healing properties and food value of aquatic plants. I have a feeling he's going to help me change the world, or at least he makes me believe I can.

We have three beautiful daughters, my love and I. We summer each year by the ocean, and I am happiest with the sea breeze in my face.

*White Bird.* Even now that we have grown old, Coyote calls me by my English name, though my people call me *'Aashaa nemeshap*. We have lived a difficult but happy life, and each day my waking thought is of thanks to have been given the choice to enter my dream world to stay.

Coyote is the last *kuseyaay* to our small band of *Kumeyaay*. We still move from place to place to evade the whites' tightfisted control and many rules. He is a wise and spiritual man, and he learned well from his grandfather about the ways of the shaman. And I have become a healer, my education complete after much study with a woman who shared with me her endless knowledge of plants and their special properties.

I am treated as though I am *Kumeyaay* by birth.

As Grandfather explained, "Sometimes it is not our blood that makes us *Kumeyaay*, but how we live and what is in our hearts."

We have three strong sons, my love and I. Every year we take them to the desert to see the very spot where their parents fell in love. There we sit near the cave, beside the pond and tell the story of how the paths of their father's vision quest and my own dreamquest crossed and brought us together to live forever.

# Author's Note

Although this story is certainly a work of fiction, I tried my best to present accurately any historical facts and time periods used. I researched extensively in order to portray the Kumeyaay people with respect, and hope my efforts were successful. My intent was to weave in the Kumeyaay language and the everyday life of the native people, creating an imaginative tale meant to entertain as well as to inform.

The setting of the Anza-Borrego Desert State Park is quite real, and if you are ever in the southern California area, you can walk the Borrego Palm Canyon Nature Trail there and visit the beautiful palm oasis where Suzanne Lucas and Coyote meet.

Mission Trails Regional Park is also real. Their visitors' center offers a look at the history of the area and contains many artifacts. Volunteers and rangers can take you to the Old Mission Dam site where Suzanne makes her final journey to return to Coyote.

The earthquake of Suzanne's youth was based on the Borrego Mountain earthquake of April 8, 1968, where the epicenter was in the Anza-Borrego park. This quake, magnitude 6.5, caused landslides and hurled large boulders downslope, damaging campers' vehicles; caused surface ruptures; and cracked Highway 78 at nearby Ocotillo Wells.

The Perseid meteor showers indeed happen each summer, in mid August. I have a favorite memory of lying in the middle of a country road, the blacktop still warm on my back, watching the stars dance across the midnight sky.

When Father Junipero Serra arrived in the San Diego area in 1769 to build the *Mission San Diego de Alcalá*, he named the peaceful native people the *Diegueños*, after the mission. The term *Kumeyaay* was historically used by the native people to describe themselves and was reinstated by Professor Florence Shipek in the 1970s. Since *Kumeyaay* is preferred, I chose to use it throughout, regardless of time period.

The difficulties Coyote's people encountered are quite real. In 1769, the Kumeyaay population was over 25,000. In 1870, the expropriation of Kumeyaay lands began; in 1871, census was 1,571. After 1910, the population began to thrive and current figures as of this printing list Kumeyaay descendants as over 20,000.

The word *shaman* would not have been used by the Kumeyaay during the time period portrayed in *Dreamquest*. Coyote's grandfather would more likely have been called *medicine man* or *healer*. I used the term in this story for its familiarity.

Plants sustained native peoples for thousands of years, providing food, tools, shelter, useful objects, and medicines. My hope is that the information within this story might prompt the reader to learn more about ethnobotany and especially the native plants of the desert. However, caution must be used when utilizing any plants for food or medicinal purposes. The jimsonweed (*Datura stramonium*) Coyote used during his vision quest is poisonous and can be deadly if ingested. This plant has long been used in ceremonies because of the plant's hallucinogenic alkaloids. People trying to imitate Native American ways have often poisoned themselves, sometimes fatally, when ingesting jimsonweed.

And finally, some acknowledgments and mentions are in order. I would like to thank some of the organizations who offer ongoing education and exhibits: American Indian Culture Center, San Diego, California; Anza-Borrego Desert State Park, Borrego

Springs, California; Barona Cultural Center and Museum, Lakeside, California; Kumeyaay-Ipai Interpretive Center at Pauwai, Poway, California; Malki Museum, Banning, California; Mission Trails Regional Park and Visitor and Interpretive Center, San Diego, California; Museum of San Diego History, San Diego, California; San Diego Historical Society, San Diego, California.

I'd like to also offer my gratitude to the many people who have generously shared of their knowledge and experience, either within the pages of books or websites, within lectures, or in personal conversations: Robert Freeman, Cheryl Hinton, Diana Lindsay, Heather Rosing, Eva Salazar, Bill White. A final homage to Dr. Florence Connolly Shipek, who tirelessly researched and advocated for the Kumeyaay people until her passing in 2003. Her 1991 updated and composite book, entitled *Delfina Cuero*, includes the autobiography of a Kumeyaay woman as told to her and interpreted by Rosalie Pinto Robertson. Delfina Cuero's story was also a source of information and inspiration for *Dreamquest*.

The primary source for the Kumeyaay language used throughout *Dreamquest* was the *Dictionary of Mesa Grande Diegueño*, by Ted Cuoro and Christina Hutcheson (native speakers); introduction and notes by Margaret Langdon, Associate Professor of Linguistics at the University of California, San Diego. The dictionary was published in 1973 by the Malki Museum Press, Morongon Indian Reservation in Banning, California.

In the 1960s, Margaret Langdon was asked to create a practical writing system for this previously almost unknown spoken language. She continued to study and analyze the Kumeyaay language for thirty years. The word *Kumeyaay* is now used to describe three closely related languages: Iipai, Kumeyaay, and Tiipai. All belong to the Yuman linguistic family, Hokan stock.

Kumeyaay was also adopted as the preferred word to describe the people who lived throughout what is now southern San Diego County and Baja California.

Pronunciation: Words are typically accented on the last syllable; an accent mark is used for unusually accented words or phrases. Words beginning with " ' " represent the sound of a catch in the throat, like the sound in the middle of the exclamation *Oh-oh!* Over time, some Spanish words were also adopted into Kumeyaay.

Other language sources used:
americanindiansource.com/kumeyaaylanguage.html
www.kumeyaay.org/words.html
www.kumeyaay.com/history/linguistics.html

I love to hear from my readers. My email address is mail@janetwellington.com.

I invite you to visit my website for more information including a bibliography of books and online sources used in my research, plus additional Kumeyaay information and helpful links: www.janetwellington.com.

# Kumeyaay Glossary

**'Aashaa nemeshap:** White Bird

**'aaskay:** pot (Sp. *olla*)

**'aaw:** fire

**Diegueño** (Sp.): This word was coined in 1769 by Father Serra to describe the indigenous people who lived close to the Mission San Diego de Alcalá. All the area Indians were referred to as Mission Indians, and later further designated by using *Diegueño*, which means "of the Diego mission"; also used to describe the language of the native people. This designation was changed by the native people in the 1970s to *Kumeyaay*.

**'ehan:** is good, correct, right, tasty, true, sure

**'Ehemach 'ewuus:** I saw it in my dreams.

**'ehpank:** whale

**'ehpii** (Sp. *metate*): A flat stone with a shallow depression used to hold grain for grinding with a hand-held stone called a (Sp.) *mano*.

**'emaa:** yucca plant (less flower and stem); shavings from the root can be used to make soapsuds

**'emat winnp:** earthquake (lit. the earth shakes)

**'emtaar:** open space, wilderness, desert, valley, yard

**'enyehaa:** my water

**'ewii taaspiich:** Sidewinder (rattlesnake found in the Anza-Borrego desert)

**haa:** yes

**háawka:** hello

**háawka 'ememaa:** hello mommy (Sp. *mama*)

**Hattepaa:** Coyote

**Hattepaa kwa'stik:** Little Coyote (coyote, the little one)

**hellyaach sekap tewaa:** half-moon

**hellytaa:** hair, head, scalp

**hemach:** dreams

**iichaa:** thinks, remembers

**kesaaw:** eat it (command)

**Kumeyaay:** The true tribal name (instead of Southern Diegueño Indians; lit. those who face the water from the cliff). These first residents of California were discovered during the mission era (1769) and inhabited the Southern California region and Baja California. In the 1950s, anthropologists discovered the native people never considered *Diegueño* their name, and *Kumeyaay* was adopted by them in the 1970s. I chose to use this preferred name for the native people in this work.

**kuseyaay:** Shaman or medicine man; kuseyaay had a great knowledge of medicine, curing songs, ceremonies, and astronomy.

**Luiseño** (Sp.): Indigenous people of what is now northern San Diego County; the name was taken from the Mission San Luis Rey. Kumeyaay used the word *Kahway* for these people.

**mes-haalyap:** butterfly

**mes-haraay:** sand

**millychish:** white man

**olla** (Sp.): pot, container

**paataat:** father

**panepaaw:** grandfather (father's father)

**ranchero** (Sp.): ranch

**Senyaweche:** Village of Kumeyaay in the area where Mission Trails Regional Park is now located in San Diego.

**shawii:** acorn mush, makes acorn mush

**shuullaw:** thunder

**simiiraay:** crazy

**temeshaa:** shadow, spirit

**tolvaach** (Sp. *toloache*): *Datura metaloides*, toxic plant commonly known as jimsonweed; of the nightshade family; has large trumpet-shaped flowers and prickly fruit; used as a tea made from leaves, stems, and roots for ceremonial and medicinal purposes. It was drunk by shamans as part of religious ceremonies and by individuals to attain personal visions.

**wekwiich:** tattoos, is tattooed